Dracula
Meets
Jack the Ripper

Other Books by
Michael B. Druxman

Fiction

ONCE UPON A TIME IN HOLLYWOOD: (A Revisionist History)
SHADOW WATCHER (Novel)
NOBODY DROWNS IN MINERAL LAKE (Novel)
CHEYENNE WARRIOR (Screenplay)

Non-Fiction

MY FORTY-FIVE YEARS IN HOLLYWOOD
and How I Escaped Alive

FAMILY SECRET (with Warren Hull)

THE ART OF STORYTELLING

THE MUSICAL: FROM BROADWAY TO HOLLYWOOD

ONE GOOD FILM DESERVES ANOTHER

CHARLTON HESTON

MERV

MAKE IT AGAIN, SAM

BASIL RATHBONE: His Life and His Films

PAUL MUNI: His Life and His Films

Plays

CLARA BOW
FLYNN
GABLE
LOMBARD
TRACY
ORSON WELLES

Dracula Meets Jack the Ripper

and Other Revisionist Histories

by Michael B. Druxman

BearManor Fiction

2011

Dracula Meets Jack the Ripper and Other Revisionist Histories

© 2011 Michael B. Druxman

For information, address:

BearManor Fiction
P. O. Box 71426
Albany, GA 31708

bearmanorfiction.com

Cover design by John Teehan
Typesetting and layout by John Teehan
Author's Photo by Elisa Ferrari

Published in the USA by BearManor Fiction

ISBN—1-59393-364-9
978-1-59393-364-7

For Sandy and David:
The two most important people in my life.

Table of Contents

Introduction 1

The Old Coot 5

Dracula Meets Jack the Ripper 13

Big Al and Desperate Dan 53

Napoleon Brandy 65

The Space Ship 101

Bugsy's Boys 107

About the Author 125

Introduction

What do you write after you've written your memoirs?

That's the question I kept asking myself even while I was still writing *My Forty-Five Years in Hollywood and How I Escaped Alive*. In fact, I probably took my time completing the book because I didn't know the answer.

Then, there was that little voice in the back of my head that kept telling me that, "when you finish your memoirs, *it's over.*"

We writers have vivid imaginations, don't we?

Ultimately, I did finish the book and it was published by Bear Manor Media in August 2010... *and I'm still here.*

How about that?

Once the manuscript had been sent off to the publisher, I went into my usual funk, the one I enter every time I finish a project and don't know what I'm going to do next.

I spent a few weeks doing some story editing for a small film production company here in Austin, and I also did some paid mentoring for a couple of writers who were trying to turn their rough ideas into workable stories. But, there was nothing of my own that I felt compelled to write.

WAS it "over"?

Years ago, I'd come up with ideas for two short stories, each one with a twist ending. They would have been perfect fodder for a half-hour series like *The Twilight Zone* or another anthology program of that ilk. I'd never written them down back then because there were no

1

anthology series on the air at that time and the market for short stories in magazines was dwindling.

As much as I love to write, my approach to writing has always been very pragmatic: If you don't think you can sell it, why bother?

That's why I had never actually written a short story before.

So, with nothing better to do after I finished my memoirs, and while I was still breathing, I decided to commit those two stories to paper.

I wrote the first draft of *The Old Coot* in November 2009, and I must admit that I really enjoyed myself. Indeed, I think that the story is one of the best things I've ever written.

Susan Artof, my publisher at The Center Press, and Frances Doel, my story editor at Roger Corman's Concorde/New Horizons, thought it was terrific. So, it was at that point that I decided that my next project would be my own book of short...*and not so short*...stories.

However, the next question to answer was:

Aside from *The Old Coot* and my other aforementioned story, *The Space Ship*, where was I going to get the rest of the stories to fill up the volume?

The answer to that was easy.

Over the years, I may have sold several of my original screenplays, but I still had a bunch of unsold scripts sitting on my shelf. The vast majority of these were good, solid stories, and the fact that they'd never been turned into a film had nothing to do with their quality. Timing, financing and the personal taste of a particular reader are just a few of the dozens of reasons why a well-written script might not get produced.

The Center Press, for example, published *Shadow Watcher* in 2007. That was my novel that I adapted from a screenplay I'd first written back in 1981.

Since both *The Old Coot* and *The Space Ship* could be classified as "revisionist histories" dealing with either real people or well-known characters from literature, I went through my scripts seeking stories that would fit into that general theme. Ultimately, I came up with four stories that, once I stripped the plot down to its basic elements, would be suitable for such a volume.

It's no secret that I was never happy with *Dillinger and Capone* (1995), the movie that Roger Corman produced based on my original screenplay, *Big Al and Desperate Dan*. The reasons are well documented in my memoir.

Luckily, I retained the publishing rights to my original screenplay, so the first of the four scripts that I chose to adapt to a short story format was that one. The "framing story" for this version may be different from my original, but I've restored what I always felt was the essence of my screenplay and the primary reason that I wrote it (i.e. to explore the relationship and basic differences between John Dillinger and Al Capone).

I've also gone back to the original title, *Big Al and Desperate Dan*.

If you've read my memoir and/or *Family Secret*, the non-fiction work that I collaborated on with Warren Hull, you will certainly recognize the genesis of *Bugsy's Boys*, originally written in 1997.

This is one of my scripts that was "in play" for a while, but even though a couple of well-known actors were interested in doing one of the two leading roles, the financing was never forthcoming.

I really enjoyed writing this one, partially because I changed the viewpoint from what was in the original script.

I like writing comedy, but working for Roger Corman and other film producers, I was never given much of an opportunity to utilize my light touch. They had no problem with my injecting moments of humor into the dramatic scripts that I wrote for them…just as long as the basic tone of the piece remained serious.

I know I can write funny. The laughs always seem to come at the right spots when one of my stage plays is produced, and *Once Upon a Time in Hollywood: From the Secret Files of Harry Pennypacker*, my 2009 book that spoofed Hollywood's Golden Era, was also well received.

But, now you can judge for yourself. Although other stories in this volume may contain moments of wit, these final two are adapted from out-and-out comedies. *Dracula Meets Jack the Ripper* is from my screenplay, *Dracula, The Ripper and Me* (1991), in which the world-renowned "vampire" meets the serial killer who terrorized London in 1888, and *Napoleon Brandy* (1999) has General Bonaparte causing mayhem when he time travels to modern day Louisiana.

Enjoy!

– **Michael B. Druxman**

The Old Coot

The boy ran. He ran just as fast as his eleven-year-old legs would carry him.

He darted around a boxcar, and then tore across two sets of railroad tracks, almost tripping when his foot slipped on the gravel between the ties.

"Stop!"

The boy heard the voice of the railroad dick behind him, but he kept on running. He knew the old bastard had a bum leg and that he wasn't going to come chasing after him or the rest of his gang when they scattered. Besides, the guy had caught the two dumb cherries that were helping them steal the coal that day, so he already had his hands full.

Stealing coal from the Pennsylvania Railroad gondolas and selling it to the neighbors was a good way to make extra dough. The boy and his gang had been doing it for months, but this was the first time that they'd been caught at it. Maybe bringing those girls along this time had been a jinx.

A blast of cool autumn wind blew dust into the boy's face, as he left the Indianapolis railroad yard and hurried down the block toward the half-alley behind the Oak Hill Tavern. Those loud-mouthed temperance speakers had been blabbing in front of the barroom earlier, but they were gone now. The boy figured that Mr. Doherty had run them off again with that club he kept behind the bar.

It was safe for the boy in the alley. He could catch his breath and wait for an hour until he was sure that the coast was clear.

He wondered if Freddy and the rest of the gang had gotten away okay.

The boy plopped down onto a wood crate in the back part of the dark, rubbish-filled alley. He took off his cap, wiped the dust from his face and spit out the few bits that had gotten into his mouth.

"Damn," he muttered. He hated being chased out of the yard and not having anything to show for it. Not even just a few pieces of coal.

Maybe he'd sneak back in a couple of hours and fill a half sack of the black rocks. That would, sure as hell, fool 'im. That railroad dick wouldn't be expecting him to come back the same day.

Meanwhile, he had to pass some time. He pulled the bent dime novel out of the back pocket of his knickers and moved the crate a bit, so that he could catch the little sunlight that managed to filter down into the half-alley.

Jesse James, Robin Hood of the West. This was the third time the boy had read the dog-eared book that had several of its pages falling out. He'd swiped it from his father's store one day while the old man was reading that stuff in the newspaper about that Archduke guy being killed in Europe, and now there was going to be a war about it.

The boy didn't really understand that. Jesse James had shot a lot of people, some of them really important, but nobody started a war over that.

Maybe that's because Jesse James was really a *good* outlaw. He robbed from the rich and gave to the poor, like that old lady who was going to lose her farm to that rotten banker. Jesse gave the lady the money to pay off her mortgage, then he stole it right back from the banker.

He was a real hero. No wonder they wrote books about him.

Maybe some day they would write a book about the boy.

The boy guffawed as he read the pages that described Jesse's early childhood and how he'd learned to handle guns. He was such a dunce at first that he even shot off a fingertip on his left hand. The boy thought that was real funny.

"What're you laughing at, sonny?"

"What?" the boy exclaimed, so startled that he jumped off the crate, tripped over his own feet and fell onto the ground.

The elderly figure rose up from the shadowy corner of the half-alley where he'd been lying behind some discarded wood crates.

"What're you sneakin' up on me like that for?" the boy said, scrambling to his feet, raising his fists in a fighter's stance. "You old coot!"

"Take it easy, sonny. Nobody's gonna hurt ya."

The boy thought this wizened-faced geezer with the long, white scraggly beard must be a hundred years old. Or, at least sixty or seventy. Either way, he was the oldest person that the boy had ever seen.

And, he must be a cowboy, because he sure dressed like one: a battered Stetson, bandana, soiled duster, torn Levis and a canvas shirt.

"What're you doin there?" the boy asked, starting to calm from his start. "Who are you?"

"Just a drifter, sonny. An 'old coot,' takin' a rest behind them crates there. I was hopin' to hop a southbound train, but the damn railroad detective threw me out of the yard. Maybe he thought I was there to steal some coal."

"Yeah?"

"By the look of yer hands, maybe that's what you've been doin', huh?"

"So, what's it to you?" the boy said, hastily rubbing his blackened hands against his knickers.

"No need to worry 'bout me, sonny. I got no love fer the railroad and the railroad certainly don't got no love fer me."

"No?"

The old coot chuckled. "No," he said. "Me and the railroads go way back." He pointed to the dime novel that had fallen to the ground. "What's that yer readin'?"

The boy scooped up the book. "It's about Jesse James," he said.

"No foolin'?"

"He was the greatest outlaw that ever lived."

"You don't say!" The old coot smiled. "It says that in that there book?"

"It sure does."

"He was greater than Billy the Kid?"

"Billy the Kid!" the boy snapped. "He weren't no Robin Hood. He was just a plain ol' killer."

"Jesse did his fair share of killin'."

"Yeah, but he just killed them crooked Northern bankers and the no good railroad men," the boy said. "They needed killin'."

"You don't say!"

"I *do* say!" the boy said, grabbing a broken brick from the ground. "And, don't you say another word 'gainst Jesse James, or I'll throw this brick at you."

"I give up," the old coot said with a chuckle. He raised his hands in a mock surrender. "Now, if you calm yourself down, I'll tell you a secret."

The boy lowered the brick. "What secret?"

"I used to ride with Jesse."

The boy's mouth dropped open, as the brick fell out of his hand. "You…you knew Jesse James?"

"Sure did."

"You…you were an outlaw?"

The old coot nodded his head.

"When?" the boy demanded. "'Cept for his brother, Frank, I thought the whole James Gang was killed or captured at Northfield."

"The Northfield bank job was sure a disaster, alright," the old coot said, sitting down onto a wood crate. "Jesse should never have gone up to Minnesota. It was too far away from home. He should've stayed in Missouri…Kentucky… or thereabouts.

"Yeah, Northfield was sure a sad day. We lost the Younger boys… Clell Miller….Everybody else who could ride just scattered."

The boy moved over to the old coot and squatted next to him. "Did you rob a lot of banks?" he asked.

"Railroads, too," the old coot said with a nod. "The Pinkertons would still be after me if they didn't think I was dead."

"They thought they got you at Northfield?"

"Or, later….See, the only way you're ever goin' to escape the law forever is to make 'em think you're dead, then go straight. That way, they stop lookin' for you."

"Jesse tried to go straight," the boy said, "but that dirty little coward shot 'im in the back."

"He did, huh?"

The boy pointed to the dime novel. "Robert Ford did it," he said. "Says so right in this book."

"Then it must be true." The old coot winked. "Gotta believe everything you read in books."

The boy wasn't quite sure what the old coot meant by that. Was he trying to tell him that the book *wasn't* true?

"So, tell me about this coal stealin' business of yours," the old coot said. "How's that work?"

"Me and my gang…."

"You got a 'gang'?" the old coot asked.

"We call ourselves The Dirty Dozen…."

The old coot chuckled. "Stealin' coal, I guess that's a good name for you."

"Yeah," the boy said, laughing at the old coot's joke, "we gotta do a lot of hand scrubbin' when we get home at night."

"Who buys this coal from you?"

"Neighbors. We sell it to 'em a lot cheaper than they can buy it from the coal dealers."

"Very enterprising," the old coot said. "And, what went wrong today?"

"It was them girls," the boy said. "Those cherries. They were beggin' us to come along. They wanted to 'help,' so Freddy says 'okay.' I didn't want to bring 'em, but Freddy says that maybe we might have some fun with them afterwards.

"The minute we got in the yard, they started yappin' and they wouldn't shut up…even after I said I'd punch 'em if they didn't shut their traps. The dick heard 'em before we even got one piece of coal. He grabbed the girls, an' me, Freddy and the rest of the gang took off.

"Dumb cherries. It'll serve them right if they spend a night in jail."

"Not very smart," the old coot said.

"I know," the boy agreed.

"I'm talkin' about *you*, sonny," the old coot said. "You're the dumb one."

Nobody called the boy "dumb". "Me?" he said, standing up, clenching his fists.

"You think those girls'll keep their yaps shut?" the old coot said. "They're goin' to point their fingers at you, an' the next thing you know, the cops are goin' to be knockin' at your door."

The boy had never thought of that.

"Why do you think that Jesse James never got caught?" the old coot asked. "Did you ever figure that out?

"Two reasons. First, he planned his jobs *himself* and he planned 'em well. He knew everything about every train, every bank and every town he ever robbed. The reason Northfield was a disaster is because he let people who weren't as smart as him do the scoutin' for him. That was his biggest mistake. He broke his own rule."

The sun was gone now. The boy was starting to feel a bit of a chill. He wished that he had his wool jacket with him.

The old coot reached into his shirt pocket, pulled out a bag of tobacco and began rolling himself a cigarette.

"What's the other reason?" the boy asked, squatting back down.

The old coot finished rolling his cigarette, and then lit it with a wood match. He took a long drag. "Friends. Neighbors," he said.

"Folks in Missouri and thereabouts hated the Northern railroads and the banks just as much as Jesse did. Them bankers were a bunch of crooks. They stole farms from honest, hard-workin' folks, so when Jesse took their money, the people didn't care. They even cheered Jesse on, and when the Pinkerton's came askin' questions, they just shook their heads and played dumb."

"That's what it says in the book," the boy said.

"Good for the book," said the old coot. "But, Jesse would never've done what you did today. He wouldn't have left them girls to be caught."

"Yeah, but…"

"No, 'buts,' sonny," the old coot interrupted. "You want folks to be loyal to you, protect you from the law? Then, you gotta do the same for them. You get me?"

The boy nodded his head. "Yes, sir, I get you."

The old coot chuckled, slapped the boy on the shoulder. "So, now you know the two most important rules about the hold-up business… *if* you should ever decide to make that your chosen profession."

He took a final drag on the cigarette, stood up and tossed it onto the ground. "Well, I gotta see if I can catch that southbound train. You think that dick is still around?"

"It's dark now," the boy said. "Most times, at night, he just sits in his shed."

"Nice talkin' to you, sonny." The old coot headed for the alley entrance.

"You know where you're goin'?" the boy asked.

"Thought I might try for California."

"Don't you have a family? Folks?"

"Sure, I do," the old coot said. "Probably got grandkids by now. But, when you're on the run, you gotta give all that up."

"But, don't the law think you're dead?"

"They do, and they will…until the day that I show up at my family's front door."

The boy studied the aged gent for a long moment, and then looked down at the dime novel.

"It's a lonely life when you're on the run, boy," the old coot said. "You should keep that in mind."

"I will."

"By the way, what's your handle?"

"Johnnie. I'm Johnnie Dillinger."

"Johnnie Dillinger," the old coot said. "I'll remember that."

"What's *your* name?" the boy asked.

"Me? I'm just an old coot."

The old coot smiled and gave a half salute with his left hand. The boy saw that the tip of one of his fingers was missing.

Before he could say anything, the old coot had disappeared into the night.

○

Dracula Meets Jack the Ripper

Bela Dracula knew that he wasn't a vampire.

Abraham Van Helsing knew that Bela Dracula wasn't a vampire.

Vampires didn't exist.

Unfortunately, the people of Transylvania didn't know that, which is why Dracula and Van Helsing had fled to England.

Dracula was sick-and-tired of sleeping in a coffin with one eye open, fearing that some gullible villager was going to sneak up on him one day and pound a wooden stake through his heart.

Besides, that local police inspector seemed to be onto their vampire scam. He'd been talking to those wealthy men with beautiful anemic young daughters, and he'd put all the pieces together.

The rich men had hired the great Professor Abraham Van Helsing to make their daughters well, but instead of prescribing a healthy diet to help their anemia, he had announced that the girls were the victims of a vampire.

Garlic would be spread throughout the bedroom. Dracula hated the smell of garlic, but he was forced to endure it in order to sneak into the bedrooms at night and give those beautiful young girls a hickey on the neck.

The next morning, Van Helsing would announce that the vampire had struck again. The search would be on, ending with the professor pounding a stake into a dummy in a coffin, which would then be consumed in flames before anybody else could get a good look at it.

Dracula and Van Helsing would then move on to the next village, where the charade would begin all over again.

Dracula wondered why these wealthy men only had beautiful young anemic daughters. Why couldn't they have beautiful young anemic sons? Putting hickeys their necks would be much more pleasant.

Van Helsing was, in fact, a medical doctor whose radical theories on anemia had been ridiculed as "Chinese medicine" and a "regression to the Dark Ages" by his colleagues in Amsterdam, but Bela had not always been a bogus vampire. He was of an aristocratic bloodline, and once he had even been an acrobat in a circus.

Unfortunately, his skin became allergic to the material in his costume, which caused him to scratch himself quite often, sometimes at the most inappropriate moments.

It was no wonder that his former partners were referred to as "the limping men."

The pair of charlatans had met in Hungary one night over several bottles of schnapps at a small village inn. Dracula had wept about his tenuous acrobatic career and Van Helsing talked about his dreams of ridding the world of anemia.

When the professor learned that the local Burgomeister's daughter was suffering from that blood disorder, he offered to treat the girl with his special diet and herbal formula, but the official refused. He and the other villagers believed the local folklore; a girl this pale had to be the victim of a vampire.

Van Helsing realized that the only way that he could help the girl was to supply and eliminate his own vampire, and that's how the partnership between the fifty-year-old "disesteemed" physician and the forty-year-old indigent aristocrat was born.

As an acrobat, Bela could move quickly, climb trellises and, best of all, he *looked* like a six-foot tall cadaver. Hence, he became the evil Count Dracula, king of the vampires, while the slightly balding, yet still handsome, more dashing Van Helsing became the renowned vampire hunter... who charged very high fees for his services, and also supplied his patients with secret doses of his herbal elixir.

The sea voyage to England had been unbearable for Dracula. While Van Helsing had relaxed in his luxurious cabin, Bela and his coffin had been locked in the ship's hold, rocking back-and-forth, back-and-forth. He had been seasick the entire trip and he had caught a cold.

In London, Van Helsing was staying at the Grand, while Dracula and his coffin were hidden out of sight in a one-room flat in the seedy Whitechapel District.

Bela hated being in Whitechapel. Not only was the fog so thick that he kept bumping into lampposts, but some fellow named "Jack the Ripper" was going around the neighborhood killing people.

"Vampires *always* live in horrid surroundings," Van Helsing had argued in defense of the housing arrangement. "In any event, soon we will both be very wealthy, and you will be able to resume your rightful place in the Romanian aristocracy."

"What good will that do me?" Bela said, holding back a sneeze. "I have become a swindler. I have defiled the name of my ancestor." He sneezed.

"Defiled the name of Vlad Dracula?" Van Helsing guffawed. "Vlad *the Impaler*!?!"

"Uncle Vlad may have had his enemies drawn and quartered and set their entrails on fire," Bela said, "but he *didn't* suck their blood."

"A true gentleman," Van Helsing said, exiting the dank room. "Now, stay inside, lie down in your casket and go to sleep like a good little vampire."

"Professor Van Helsing?"

Inspector Trevor Griggs approached Van Helsing, as he arrived back at the Grand. The detective, a Cockney, was endowed with a wrestler's build, the face of a bulldog and he walked with a slight limp.

"Yes?" Van Helsing replied with an indifferent tone. "What is it?"

"Sir, I'm with Scotland Yard. I'm here to follow up on a report we've received from the Transylvanian authorities about you and 'this Dracula chap.'"

"How interesting," Van Helsing said.

"I'm sorry to trouble you, sir," Griggs said. "I can see that you are a gentleman. Here we got this Jack the Ripper chap terrorizing London, and the Super keeps wasting an experienced detective like me on something trivial like this."

"Absolutely shameful," Van Helsing said.

"Know what he had me doing last week? Had me chasing a chimpanzee that escaped from the Barnum and Bailey circus in town."

"Hope he didn't make a monkey out of you," Van Helsing said.

"What's that?"

"I said, 'Your Super should make better use of you.'"

"That he should," Griggs said. Van Helsing headed into the hotel. "Professor, what should I tell my Super?"

"I should tell him the truth," Van Helsing said, as he disappeared through the doors.

"Right!" Griggs said, not quite sure what had just happened.

An hour later, Van Helsing was enjoying his supper in the hotel's dining room.

"Aren't you Professor Abraham Van Helsing?"

"I am, sir," Van Helsing said to the slim, younger man in the Chesterfield coat and black silk hat who was standing next to his table.

"I'm Doctor John Seward. I attended a lecture you gave at Cambridge. Your theories on anemia were…revolutionary."

"Perhaps a bit *too* revolutionary," Van Helsing said, inviting his colleague to sit.

"Don't be too disheartened, Professor," Seward said. "Look how long it's taken for Pasteur's theories to be accepted."

"Yes, but Pasteur is a Frenchman."

Van Helsing sipped his wine. "Do you have a patient here at the hotel?" he asked the doctor.

"In a manner of speaking," Seward said. "I'm on staff at the Burgoyne Hospital, and I'm at the hotel to reclaim a patient named Renfield who escaped from the hospital's mental ward and had, somehow, managed to register at the Grand."

"Enterprising fellow."

"Two years ago," Steward explained, "the man was a janitor at the British Museum, and now he believes he's Queen Victoria."

"Amazing," Van Helsing said. "Opportunities in England these days are endless."

Behind them, two strapping hospital attendants in white coats escorted a tall, lumbering bearded man, attired in a matronly dress, through the lobby and out the front doors of the hotel. "Where's Albert?" the man shouted. "I want Albert."

"Professor," Seward said, "if you have time, there's another patient I'd like you to examine."

"Anemia?"

"The family is quite wealthy, friends of Sir Gerald Crofton."

"Who?"

"Our chief of staff. They would certainly make it very worth your while."

Van Helsing offered Seward a glass of port. "In that case," he said, "it would be my pleasure."

Dracula sneezed. He paced his room, and then sneezed again.

He took a swig from a bottle of medicine that Van Helsing had left with him, and then spit it out. "He's trying to poison me," he said, throwing the bottle across the room. Another sneeze.

What he needed was *schnapps*!

The Jews might have their chicken soup, but his cure-all was schnapps!

Bela didn't care what Van Helsing had said. He was tired of being stuck in this room. He grabbed his cape and black silk hat. He was going out to a pub and, like "a good little vampire," he would suck the schnapps from the living.

He would even take his false vampire fangs with him. He'd feel naked going out without them.

Dracula walked two blocks until he encountered Bailey's Pub, located on a corner at Whitechapel Road. As usual, it was filled with a loud, boisterous crowd, mostly laborers, arguing, arm wrestling, pushing, shoving and drinking plenty of ale.

At one end of the bar, Harry Cox, a burly, loquacious gent in a moth-eaten cap and haggard suit was holding court with three other men and Sally, a buxom tart wearing too much makeup. "I say, the Ripper don't come from nowhere near Whitechapel," Cox said. "He's probably one of them bloody toffs that come down here at night to have their way with our women."

"It's gettin' so a lady can't walk the streets alone at night," Sally said, picking her nose.

Arthur T. Bailey, the wiry proprietor/bartender who sported a handlebar mustache, delivered a glass and a bottle of his finest spirits to the corner booth where Dracula sat in his evening clothes. "That's all they talk about these days," Bailey said to his new customer. "Jack the Ripper! Jack the Ripper!" He displayed the bottle of liquor. "Best in the house, Guv."

Dracula corrected him. "Count," he said, and then he sneezed.

"What?"

"I am *not* a governor. I am a Count."

"Whatever you say, Guv. You want the bracer or not?"

"Leave the bottle." Dracula said, tossing coins onto the table. Bailey scooped up the money and walked away. "Peasant," Dracula muttered under his breath.

Bela had finished about a third of the bottle when Sally, looking for some business, sauntered over to his booth. "You *really* a Count, Dearie?" she inquired.

"I am Count Bela Dracula of Transylvania," he said with drunken dignity. "Last living descendent of Prince Vlad Dracula."

"A real gent, eh?" Sally said, quite impressed. "Course the fella spoutin' off at the bar thinks that the ol' Ripper is a gent, too."

"A kindred spirit," Dracula said. He sipped his drink.

"You have a castle, and…?"

"There *is* a family castle."

"*Blimey!*" Sally said. "Never had me a Count before."

"I beg your pardon?"

"Wanna buy me a drink?" she said, sliding into the booth next to him.

"Certainly," Dracula said, resigned to the fact that she wasn't going to leave. He called to Bailey, "*Innkeeper!*"

Bailey responded by bringing a mug of beer over to the table.

"Bet you're a rich one, you are?" Sally said to Bela. She gave him a playful poke.

"Please. Do not touch me!"

"Sorry, Dearie."

"Alas," Bela said, "I am sorry to say, I come from the poor side of the family." He downed another drink.

"The poor side?"

"As a Dracula, I should be eating caviar and drinking champagne…"

"We'd have to go someplace else for that, Dearie," Sally said, taking a swallow of beer.

"But instead," Dracula said to himself with disgust, "I must drink blood."

Caught by surprise, Sally started to choke. She spit out her beer in a wide spray.

"Hey!" Bailey called from behind the bar. "None of that here!"

"You drink *what!?!*" Sally said to Dracula.

"I drink blood," he said with a grin that exposed his false fangs.

Sally screamed. She scooted away and, in doing so, fell off her seat onto the floor. Bailey hurried over and pulled her to her feet. "All right, Sal," he said. "We'll have none of the rough stuff in here tonight."

"But," she protested hysterically, as he escorted her toward the door, "he's…he's the bloody…!"

"He's a bloody Count," Bailey interrupted. "I know."

"No! He's…," but before she could say another word, Sally was out the door. "He's the bloody goddamn Ripper, he is," she shouted, as the door slammed shut.

Nobody heard her. Gathering what was left of her pride, she stomped down the fog-filled street. "I'll find me a bloody bobbie," she muttered to herself.

She did not see the obscure figure of the man dressed in evening clothes and carrying a doctor's bag who stepped out of the shadows and began to follow her.

Inside the pub, Bela had taken note of Jimmy, a tall, sallow, delicately handsome young man, who was sitting at the bar, listening to Harry Cox's rant. He finished his bottle, rose from his table with a drunken flourish and, as he headed for the door, he stopped and studied Jimmy's long white neck. "Good evening," he said to the young man.

Jimmy, no genius, responded, "Yeah?"

"You don't have anemia, do you?" Dracula asked, inadvertently exhibiting his grotesque false fangs.

"Christ almighty!" Jimmy blanched and, thinking of nothing better to do, hauled off and punched Dracula in the eye.

Dracula staggered backward, crashed out through the front door. Jimmy strolled over and slammed the door shut, and then sauntered back to the bar. "Bloody toff!" he said.

Bailey grabbed a sawed-off wooden persuader from under the bar and smashed Jimmy over the head with it. "You bloody boob," he said. "He was a *payin'* customer."

Outside, a stunned Dracula picked himself up from the ground and felt his swelling eye. "Peasants!" he muttered, attempting to stagger down the foggy street toward his flat. "Uncle Vlad had the right idea. Draw them! Quarter them! Set fire to their entrails! And then… kill them! Dead! After which, you piss on their graves."

He stopped next to an alley entrance, unbuttoned his trousers and relieved himself against the brick wall. Standing there, he flashed his false fangs in anger, and then emitted a low growl.

From the obscurity of the mist in the alley, his utterance was returned with the sound of another human growl.

Bela looked about, frightened and quickly buttoned up his pants.

There was a movement in the alley. Dracula spun around and, on the mist-covered-ground, he saw a woman's feet sprawled in either direction.

He blanched, which considering his normal pallor, was quite a feat.

Then, he moved forward for a closer look.

It was the bloodied body of a woman. Sally, the woman in the pub. She had been stabbed, gutted. Her face exhibited a look of absolute terror.

Another growl. A man, about fifty, stepped out of the mist and stood next to the body. He was wearing evening clothes. In one hand he carried a doctor's bag and, in the other, a bloodied scalpel. He glowered at Dracula.

Unnerved, Bela swallowed hard. He found it difficult to speak. Attempting a smile, he asked, "Ripper?"

The man nodded. "Ripper."

Bela began to tremble with fear. Unable to think of anything better to do, he flashed his false fangs, pointed to them and said, "Va… Vampire."

The Ripper was momentarily taken aback.

Then, Dracula's trembling shook his false fangs loose and they fell from his mouth. He caught them.

The Ripper smiled. "Really?" he said, raising his scalpel and taking a step toward Dracula, who backed away, turned and ran back toward Bailey's. The Ripper started after him.

Dracula ran past the pub entrance, just as the door opened. He did not stop, but continued to run down the street, cape flying in his breeze.

An inebriated Harry Cox and Jimmy emerged from the pub, observing Dracula as he disappeared around a corner. "Hey," Cox said, "weren't that the bloody Count?"

Spotting the two men, The Ripper halted his pursuit of Dracula, ducked into a doorway.

"What bloody Count?" Jimmy asked.

"The one you boffed in the beezer," Cox said, moving up the street in The Ripper's direction.

"Didn't boff 'im in the beezer," Jimmy said. "Boffed 'im in the bloody jellies."

"You boffed 'im in the bloody jellies?"

As the men drew closer, The Ripper backed away. He hurried up the street and disappeared into the fog.

"The bloody jellies." Jimmy said.

"Serves the toff right," Cox said. He stopped, noticing something on the ground. "Hold on! What's this?"

It was a woman's feet sprawled in either direction.

Dracula ran down one fog-shrouded street and up the next. He kept glancing over his shoulder, hoping that he'd lost The Ripper.

Actually, it was Bela who was lost among the maze of streets in Whitechapel. It took him over four hours and a hard encounter with a lamppost, which blackened his other eye, before he found his way back to the safety of his hotel.

"My God!" he thought as he climbed the three flights of stairs to his room. "I saw The Ripper...*and he saw me!*"

He wished that he had never left Transylvania.

The only illumination in his room was from the street. Dracula locked the door behind him, and then leaned against it while he caught his breath. His swollen eyes began to adjust to the darkness, and he saw:

The silhouette of a man, sitting in a chair.

Dracula jumped with fright. He tried to scream, but his voice was gone, the victim of his panic.

The man stood up. He started moving toward Dracula.

Dracula turned back toward the door, and tried to pull it open, but it was locked.

"Bela, where have you been?" Van Helsing said.

The voice didn't register with Dracula. Still attempting a scream, he tried harder to pull open the door, but with no better result.

"Bela!" Van Helsing put his hand on his shoulder.

Dracula froze, still not recognizing the voice. He did not turn around. Instead, he took the only course left open to him. He fainted.

When Bela opened his eyes a few minutes later, he was lying on the bed and Van Helsing was standing over him, holding smelling salts under his nose. "Come, Bela," the professor said, "there's work to do."

Dracula smiled slightly at his partner, and then suddenly remembered the night's terrifying events. He bolted upright, grabbed the front of Van Helsing's coat and opened his mouth to speak.

"Aaahhh…!" No discernable sound emerged from his still frozen vocal cords.

"My God! Your breath is ghastly!" Van Helsing said, removing Dracula's hands from his coat.

"Aaahhh…!"

"Now, look at you," Van Helsing scolded. "You've gone and developed a spot of laryngitis. I told you to stay inside…take the medicine I gave you."

Frustrated, Dracula leaped off the bed and stomped around the room, making stabbing motions with his hand, tying to pantomime Jack the Ripper. "Aaahhh! Asshhh…!"

"What are you doing?" Van Helsing asked.

Dracula continued to pantomime, hand upraised like he was holding a knife, as he stalked toward Van Helsing.

"Would you stop this silliness?" Van Helsing said. He took the struggling, silently protesting Dracula by the arm, escorted him over to the washbasin and poured in some water from the pitcher. "Clean yourself up! We have a patient to see."

Dracula looked at Van Helsing with disbelief.

"Miss Mina DeKooning," Van Helsing said. "Her parents are *very* wealthy. And, if all goes well, she may be our last case." He handed Dracula a washcloth. "Now, wash!"

Fifteen minutes later, Van Helsing and Dracula walked out of the hotel and headed up the foggy street toward Whitechapel Road. While Van Helsing kept his eyes peeled for a cab, Dracula kept glancing around to make sure that they were not being followed.

"You only have to be in her room for a moment," Van Helsing said. "Just long enough to plant that purple mark onto her neck."

Bela, still unable to speak, responded with a disgusted, "Aaaggh…"

"You don't have to *bite* her," Van Helsing said. "Just *suck* the neck… like with the others. Actually, I understand that women find that to be a rather pleasurable sensation."

Reaching an intersection, Van Helsing spotted a Hansom cab and hailed it with his walking stick. As the two men hurried toward the vehicle, The Ripper stepped out of a shadowy doorway, watched them for a moment, and then began to follow.

Scotland Yard's Chief Inspector Harrison and his boss, Superintendent McNamara, were already present when Inspector Griggs arrived at the crime scene by Bailey's Pub. McNamara knew that Griggs was the most incompetent detective on his force, but he couldn't really fire him because, five years earlier, Griggs had saved the superintendent's life when he'd pulled him out of the way of a runaway carriage. That's how Griggs had gotten his limp.

"Evenin', sir," Griggs said. "Nasty business, what?"

McNamara forced himself to smile. "I thought you were assigned to Waterloo tonight."

"I saw my man, sir," Griggs said. "Professor chap. I think he's all right."

"Good to know the Empire's safe," Harrison muttered under his breath.

"I heard the Ripper'd struck again," Griggs said to McNamara. "I figured you could use all the help down here you could get. Want me to survey the crime scene? See if I can come up with some clues?"

"NO!" McNamara and Harrsion spoke in unison.

McNamara put his hand on Grigg's shoulder. "Go inside the pub," he said. "Have a drink. Have several. See what you can learn from the patrons."

"Good idea," Griggs said. "I'll report to you personally, sir."

"Please do," the superintendent said facetiously.

"Wouldn't it be easier just to retire him, sir?" Harrison asked, as he watched Griggs limp off toward the pub. "I mean, with pension?"

"I've tried that," McNamara said.

"And...?"

"He cried."

Inside the pub, Griggs took a gulp of his second beer, as he pondered what Bailey and his patrons had told him. "This toff that Sally was talkin' to," he asked, "what'd he look like?"

"Tall," Bailey said. "Dressed elegant. He was a foreigner."

"How do you know that?"

"Talked with an accent. A foreign one."

"Had the nastiest teeth, he did," Harry Cox interjected. "Tried to bite Jimmy here on the neck."

"I gave 'im what for," Jimmy said, raising his fist.

"Anybody catch his name?" Griggs asked.

"Foreign name," Bailey said.

"Figured," Griggs said.

"He was a duke or earl or somethin'," Cox said.

"Dracula!" Bailey said. "That's it! Count Dracula."

"Dracula!?!" Griggs said, his mouth hanging agape.

Fog surrounded the Burgoyne Hospital, as Van Helsing and Dracula approached the left wing of the building. "That's the one," the professor said, pointing to a window on the third floor. "The one next to the trellis. It's unlatched."

"Aaaahhh…," Bela said.

Van Helsing took Bela by the arm and led him over to the trellis. "Up you go," he said.

Dracula hesitated.

"Don't dawdle!" Van Helsing said with a yawn. "I want to get back to my hotel. Do you want me to be tired when I visit my patient in the morning?" He poked Dracula with his walking stick. "Now, Up! Up! Up!"

Dracula gave Van Helsing a nasty look, and then put his foot onto the bottom rung of the trellis. The rotten wood broke; causing him to fall forward, bump his head against the brick wall.

"What are you doing?" Van Helsing scolded. "Trying to wake up the whole hospital?"

Dracula, a slight bruise on his forehead, glowered at Van Helsing, and then started up the trellis again, this time with better luck. "That's the idea!" the professor said, turning to leave. "When you finish here, you can go home, lie in your coffin and sleep the day away." As he strolled off toward the street, Dracula made an obscene gesture in his direction.

Van Helsing crossed the street and turned a corner, looking for a cab. He did not see The Ripper come out of the fog behind him and start toward the hospital.

Bela continued to climb slowly up the trellis, muttering to himself in wordless grunts of anger, while grasping onto the thin vines for support. He reached the barred second floor window and momentarily paused.

Renfield's bewildered, wide-eyed pale face suddenly appeared on the other side of the glass. Startled, Dracula opened his mouth in a soundless frightened cry, as he lost his balance and fell to the ground.

"Albert?" Renfield said, peering out the window.

Dracula lay flat on his back for a moment, and then started to pick himself up. Glancing toward the street, he saw the fog silhouetted figure of The Ripper, medical bag in hand, rapidly approaching him.

Dracula blanched. He opened his mouth to scream, but again, there was no sound. He leapt to his feet, grabbed onto the trellis and scurried up toward the third floor window.

Renfield's eyes followed him as he soared past. "Albert!" he said.

Dracula reached the third floor window and nudged it open. Pushing hard against the wood trellis, he vaulted through the window and fell inside.

His action broke the trellis' supports. The wood structure tumbled away from the building and crashed down upon the ground, forcing The Ripper to jump out of its way.

In his padded room on the second floor, Renfield, still in his matron's dress, rushed to the locked door, calling "Albert's here!"

He spotted a large spider crawling up the wall next to the doorframe. "Dinner!" he beamed. He grabbed the creature, popped it into his mouth and swallowed it with one quick gulp. Then, he turned back to the door. "Albert's here!" he shouted. "Albert's here!"

In the dark, small, austere patient's room on the floor above, Dracula picked himself up off of the floor and peered out the window.

On the ground below, The Ripper was staring up at the window, a malevolent smile on his face. After a moment, the killer turned and headed toward the front of the hospital.

Pondering an escape route, Dracula tiptoed toward the door, opened it a crack and peeked outside. An auburn-haired nurse in her mid-thirties was seated directly across from him, reading a magazine.

As he shut the door, he heard a moan behind him. He spun around and, for the first time, saw the patient, Mina DeKooning, stirring in her bed. From the moonlight spilling in from the window, Bela could see that she was a lovely, blond-haired girl about twenty, who had a look of innocence about her. She moaned again.

Afraid that the nurse would hear, Dracula moved frantically to the bed; put his finger to his lips and made "Shhh" noises. Mina, unaware of his presence, fell back into a deep sleep.

Dracula stared at the girl's naked neck. He hated what he was about to do, but the sooner he did it, the sooner he could contemplate his escape. Resigned, he licked his lips, raised his cape and delivered a hickey that only a vampire king could give.

Mina opened her eyes slightly, smiled, and then returned to her peaceful slumber.

The Ripper rounded the side of the building and entered the hospital through the front doors. The lobby was empty, as he moved down the corridor and headed up the main staircase.

"I want Albert!" Renfield's cry echoed throughout the second floor.

The Ripper saw Holmwood, a hospital orderly, coming out of the supply closet, carrying a straightjacket. "Evenin', sir!" Holmwood said to The Ripper. "Bit late for you to be here, ain't it?" He didn't wait for a response, but hurried down the corridor toward Renfield's room.

The Ripper continued up the stairs to the third floor. The nurse with auburn hair, Miss O'Herlihy, was seated outside of his patient's door, reading a magazine. "Sir Gerald," she said, rather surprised. She stood and did a slight curtsy. "What are you doing here at this hour?"

Sir Gerald Crofton, chief of staff at Burgoyne Hospital, doffed his hat and cape, and tossed them over a chair. "Checking on my patient," he said, looking over Mina DeKooning's medical chart. "Her father, after all, is a dear old friend."

Inside of Mina's room, Dracula heard the voices on the other side of the door and began to panic. He moved to the window and looked out. With the trellis gone, there would be no escape there.

"Get away from me, you stupid oaf!" Renfield's voice could be heard clearly from the floor below.

"Your Majesty," Holmwold said, as he, straightjacket in hand, pursued the frantic Renfield around the small padded room, "it's just your sleeping jacket."

"Poppycock!" Renfield shouted. "Rot! Rubbish! Bullshit!"

"Now, your Majesty…." Holmwood made a jump toward the patient, missed and fell over the bed. Renfield grabbed the metal washbasin from the side table; brought it down hard onto the orderly's head and, with a loud *Bong*, knocked him unconscious.

"That will teach you to lie to your queen, you dimwitted asshole!" Renfield said.

In the room above, Dracula thought he heard The Ripper's voice on the other side of the door. "Have you been here all evening, Miss O'Herlihy?" Sir Gerald Crofton asked.

Dracula's eyes darted around the room, searching for a hiding place.

"Been sittin' so long, I've nearly finished me magazine," Nurse Lucy O'Herlihy said, as the door began to open.

"You don't really believe that foolishness in those occult magazines, do you?" Crofton chuckled. The door opened further.

Dracula dove under the bed.

"I certainly do," Nurse O'Herlihy said. "Ever since I was five, and woke up to find a leprechaun sittin' at the foot of me bed."

Rather than going to the bed, Crofton stood in the doorway, surveying the room for signs of an intruder. "Who left this window open?" he asked, crossing to the window and shutting it. Underneath Mina's bed, Dracula lay very still, trying to make himself very small.

"It was probably Dr. Seward's friend," the nurse replied.

"Dr. Seward's friend?" Crofton walked over to the wardrobe and glanced inside.

"Yes, sir. He was a specialist, he was. A professor."

"His name?"

"Van Helsing."

Puzzled as to where the intruder might be hiding, Crofton moved away from the wardrobe door, neglecting to close it completely. "Van Helsing?" he said aloud to himself, trying to remember where he'd heard the name before.

"Sir," the nurse said, "didn't you want to check the patient?"

"Of course," Crofton said. He walked over to the bed and took Mina's pulse. As he pretended to examine the sleeping girl, he glanced downward. The intruder *couldn't* be hiding underneath the bed, could he?

Crofton was about to risk embarrassment; stoop down and look under the bed, when:

"Patient escaped!" Holmwood's voice echoed down the corridor.

Both Nurse O'Herlihy and Crofton turned their attention toward the door. Behind them, Dracula rolled out from underneath the bed and ducked into the wardrobe, quietly closing the door.

Sensing the movement, Crofton spun around, but saw nothing. Quickly, he stooped down, glanced under the bed.

"He's escaped again!" Holmwood shouted, the sound of his voice closer.

"Is something wrong, sir?" Nurse O'Herlihy asked.

"No...I..." Crofton said, standing, somewhat embarrassed. "When I was coming into the hospital a few minutes ago, I thought I saw...the patient at her window."

"Haven't heard a sound, sir," the nurse said.

"Quite," Crofton said. He looked over at the wardrobe again.

"He's out!" Holmwood appeared at the door, strapped into his own straightjacket.

"Good God!" Crofton said. "Not Renfield again." He crossed over to the door, and then turned back to Nurse O'Herlihy. "Perhaps Miss DeKooning has been walking in her sleep. Stay in here with her. Don't move from her side."

"I won't, sir," Nurse O'Herlihy said.

"I'll be back in the morning." He glanced back at the wardrobe, and then shut the door to the room behind him, joining Holmwood in the corridor. "What happened?" he asked the orderly, helping him out of the straightjacket.

"It's 'Her Majesty' again, sir," Holmwood said.

"A charity patient...of minimum intelligence...yet he gives this hospital more trouble than the Dervishes gave Gordon at Khartoum."

"Yes, sir."

"Post an orderly at every door. I want this hospital totally secured until this madman is found. Is that understood?"

"Indeed, sir," Holmwood said.

Crofton handed the orderly the straightjacket, and then headed for his office. "Van Helsing," he mused to himself, as he strolled down the corridor.

Inside Miss DeKooning's room, Bela peeked out through the cracks between the wardrobe doors. The nurse was sitting next to the sleeping patient, reading her magazine. He was trapped. Resigned to the fact that he was going to be there for a while, he slowly and quietly sank down into a sitting position and shut his eyes.

Following a sound night's sleep and a hearty breakfast of sausage and eggs, Van Helsing strolled out of the Grand Hotel, carrying his medical bag and walking stick, to find Inspector Griggs waiting for him. "Morning, Professor," the detective said.

"Inspector," Van Helsing replied, heading for a Hansom cab.

"Thought we might finish our talk about your friend, Count Dracula."

"You did, did you?"

"There was another Ripper murder last night in Whitechapel."

"Terrible!" Van Helsing said, as the hotel doorman opened the cab door for him. "You should be out catching the man."

"That's what I'm doing," Griggs said. "Witnesses at the scene have identified your Count Dracula chap as bein' the Ripper."

"What!?!" Van Helsing held back a smile.

"He was seen followin' the victim out of the pub just before she was done in."

"Dracula is The Ripper!?!" Van Helsing could not help himself. He burst out laughing.

"That's what it looks like," Griggs said, taken aback by the professor's reaction. "Now, could I ask you about your relationship with this Count Dracula?"

"Certainly," Van Helsing said, signaling the cab driver to proceed. "You could ask."

The cab pulled away from the curb, leaving the detective with his mouth agape. Griggs didn't notice the tall, ungainly beanpole of a man with bright red hair, dressed in an Inverness-style coat, who had stopped on the street next to him and was also watching the departing vehicle.

Van Helsing was met at the hospital entrance by Dr. Seward, who escorted him past the orderly guarding the front door. "Renfield broke out again last night," the doctor said, explaining the security. "They think he's still in the building."

"Truly a resourceful fellow, isn't he?" Van Helsing said.

"Very."

"By the way, doctor," Van Helsing said as they started up the stairs, "do I submit my bill through you, or..."

Inside of Mina DeKooning's hospital room, the patient was still asleep and Nurse O'Herlihy was dozing in her chair.

The wardrobe door opened a crack and a haggard Dracula, with an aching back from his night in the cramped quarters, poked his head out. He figured that the coast was as clear as it was going to be, so he stepped out of the closet, closing its door quietly behind him. As he tiptoed toward the door of the room, Mina moaned in her sleep.

Dracula froze; he looked over at the girl. Her eyes were closed, and the nurse was still dozing. He moved quickly, quietly to the door and opened it.

Looking to his right up the corridor, he saw a nurse and orderly checking items in a supply closet. No escape there.

Glancing in the opposite direction, he spotted Van Helsing and another man rounding the corner and heading directly toward him. He ducked back inside the room and closed the door.

"Hello?" Mina said.

Dracula looked over at the bed. Mina's eyes were open, expressing an innocent curiosity at him. He could only respond with a silly, awkward grin.

"Have you been to a party?" she asked, noting his evening clothes.

Dracula nodded. He could hear voices in the corridor, and they were drawing nearer. He looked over at the wardrobe again.

"I like parties," Mina said. "I don't go to many since I became ill...."

"What's that, sir?" Nurse O'Herlihy said. Her eyes were closed but she was starting to awaken.

In a panic, Dracula put his finger to his lips, "Shhh!"

There was a knock at the door. Nurse O'Herlihy's eyes started to open, and Dracula made a quick dive under the bed.

"Nurse?" Mina said, bewildered at this turn of events.

Nurse O'Herlihy turned to her patient; gathered herself together. "Yes, dear?"

"There's a maitre d' under my bed!"

Another knock at the door. "Now, dear," Nurse O'Herlihy said, as she went to open it, "you know that's just another of your bad dreams. Last week, you were being attacked by giant bullfrogs."

"But, this one was so real."

Under the bed, Bela didn't move. He breathed a sigh of relief and thanked God for creating giant bullfrogs.

"Good morning, Miss O'Herlihy," Dr. Seward said, as he and Van Helsing entered the room. "Is our patient up?"

"Yes, doctor."

"Mina, this is Professor Van Helsing," Seward said. "He's an expert on anemia, and I've asked him to examine you."

The professor took the girl's pulse. "My, but you're a pretty one," he said, then, "How did you get this mark?" He pointed to the welt on her neck.

"I...I don't know."

"I've never seen it before, Professor," Nurse O'Herlihy said.

"Doctor, take a look at this," Van Helsing said.

"That is unusual," Seward said, examining the welt. "Mina, you didn't stick yourself with a brooch, did you?"

"No."

"It's a bite," Van Helsing announced. "Nurse, get me a basket full of garlic."

"Garlic, sir?" Nurse O'Herlihy said.

"Garlic."

"Yes, sir," she said and scurried out of the room.

Van Helsing lowered his voice, moving Seward away from the bed. "The girl," he said, "has become the victim of the most vicious, evil creature on the face of the earth, Count Dracula."

"Who?"

"A vampire!"

"A vampire!?!" Seward couldn't believe what he was hearing.

"And," Van Helsing said, "if we do not save her, she will become his next disciple, his bride."

Seward took a step backward and wondered if Professor Abraham Van Helsing should join Renfield, when they caught him, in the mental ward. "Professor," he said, trying to be tactful, "don't you think...?"

"He's right, Seward."

Seward and Van Helsing turned to see Sir Gerald Crofton standing in the doorway.

Under the bed, Dracula seemed to recognize the new voice, but he didn't know from where.

"Professor Van Helsing knows all about the undead," Crofton continued. He entered the room and extended his hand to the professor. "You see, I've traveled extensively through the Balkans."

"Sir Gerald is our chief of staff," Seward said.

"I'm quite aware of your pursuit of this Count Dracula," Crofton said. "I've also read your research on anemia, and I must say that, unlike some of my colleagues, I find it to be rather interesting."

"Thank you," Van Helsing said.

"Please proceed with your examination, Professor," Crofton said, and then noting the dubious expression on Seward's face, "It will be all right, doctor."

"Professor," Mina said, "am I going to be…?"

"You are going to be fine, my dear," Van Helsing said. He moved back over to the bed and took hold of her hand. "*If* you do exactly as I tell you." He produced a small crucifix on a gold chain from his pocket. "I want you to wear this at all times. *Never* take it off."

"But, Professor," Mina protested, "I'm Jewish."

"That's all right." Van Helsing said. "Dracula is non-denominational."

He placed the crucifix around her neck, and then turned to Crofton and Seward. "A vampire fears the Cross."

"What if he's an atheist?" asked Crofton.

"That's why we use garlic as a back-up," Van Helsing said. "Stinks to high heaven." He opened his medical bag and took out a small bottle. "Nurse!"

Nurse O'Herlihy appeared immediately at the door, carrying a plate full of garlic bulbs. "Yes, sir," she said.

"Give the patient a half teaspoon of these herbs, mixed with tea, every three hours."

"What are they?" Seward asked.

"Chinese herbs. They will strengthen her blood, and also act as a repellant to the vampire."

"Should repel people, too," Nurse O'Herlihy said, sniffing the bottle.

Van Helsing scowled at her. "Spread the garlic bulbs around the windows," he said, "and the bed."

"Whatever you say, sir." Her eyes expressed her doubts.

Van Helsing suddenly felt a tug on his trouser leg. The two physicians, who were watching Nurse O'Herlihy placing the garlic at the window, failed to note the brief look of surprise in his eyes.

The professor looked down to see Dracula's cadaver-like hand beckoning him from under the bed. "*Just* the windows, nurse," he said, dropping his pencil onto the floor. "Clumsy me!"

He ducked down, ostensibly to retrieve the pencil, and looked under the bed.

Dracula grimaced foolishly at him. Van Helsing's mouth dropped.

"Professor?" Crofton said.

Van Helsing glowered at his partner, and then grabbing the pencil, "Here it is!" He stood up, too quickly, bumping his head on the underside of the bed.

On his feet, he hastily composed himself and saw that Crofton was about to take a peek under the bed. "Gentlemen," he said, escorting both doctors toward the door, "let's adjourn to another room where we can discuss a further course of treatment."

He turned back to the nurse. "I think the patient could use some exercise. Why don't you take her for a little stroll? A *long* little stroll."

"But," Seward protested, "what about this Count Dracula? Shouldn't…?"

"Don't worry," Van Helsing interrupted, raising his voice and directing it toward the bed. "Vampires are never seen in the daylight."

Under the bed, Dracula got the message.

"Tell me, Professor," Crofton said, as he sat behind the desk in his office, "what does this Count Dracula look like?"

"He's rather tall, aristocratic…."

"Moronic-looking?" Crofton interjected.

"Yes," Van Helsing said absently, his mind still focused under Mina's bed. "As a matter of fact, he…."

"No!" he hastily caught himself. "He…He's a very clever adversary. You haven't seen him, have you?"

Crofton shook his head. "And, once we find him, how do we deal with this…fiend?" he asked.

"Call in Scotland Yard," Seward suggested.

"You say he fears the Cross," Crofton said. "How about the Archbishop of Canterbury? He's a personal friend."

"Gentlemen," Van Helsing said, standing up and beginning to pace the room, "all that is useless. We must track Dracula to his lair, find him sleeping in the coffin filled with his native soil, and drive a stake through his heart."

Seward's reaction was a look of disgust. He looked across the desk at Crofton.

"That's rather…messy, isn't it?" Crofton said with a smile. "Wouldn't a simple bullet do?"

"*A stake*, gentlemen!" Van Helsing said.

"Fine," Crofton said. "Now that we know how to kill the Count, how do we find him?"

"Follow him," Van Helsing said. "I will be in Miss DeKooning's room tonight to protect her. You and Seward will wait outside the building and pursue him back to his hiding place."

"What if he turns himself into a bat?" Crofton said. "Tracking him would be rather difficult."

"Vampires only transform themselves on special occasions," Van Helsing said. "Like All Hallows Eve and Friedrich Nietzsche's birthday."

"Why can't some of the orderlies wait outside?" Seward asked. "It's bloody cold, you know."

"The less people who know about this the better." Van Helsing's eyes fell onto a large portrait of a handsome, sour-faced, stately woman in her fifties, hanging on the wall behind Crofton's desk.

"The Professor's right," Crofton said. "Have to protect the good name of the hospital."

"Lady Crofton?" Van Helsing asked, admiring the portrait.

"My mother," Crofton replied.

"Striking woman."

"She was," Crofton said, his face twitching slightly.

"Reminds me of *my* mother. She was also a striking woman," Van Helsing said. "Striking me on the head, striking me on the backside…"

He shook his head, and then walked out of the room, leaving the two physicians exchanging looks of bewilderment.

Van Helsing returned to Mina DeKooning's room to find the patient, back from her short exercise, sipping her prescribed herbal tea and Nurse O'Herlihy placing the last of the garlic bulbs around the windows. "How's the tea," he asked, as he felt the girl's pulse and wondered if Dracula had had a chance to make his escape.

"Bitter," Mina said.

"Good things often are." He let his pencil drop to the floor. "My, but I'm clumsy today!" He stooped down to retrieve the pencil, took a quick peek under the bed and then, relieved to find nobody there, stood back up.

"Professor," Mina said, "am I ever going to get well?"

"My dear, Miss Mina," Van Helsing said, his attention drawn to the wardrobe, "I guarantee you that if you follow my instructions for one month, you will feel like a new person." He strolled over to the wardrobe, opened it and looked inside, "My, but they have interesting wardrobes in British hospitals."

"What kind of wardrobes do they have in European hospitals, Professor?" Nurse O'Herlihy asked, her eyes again expressing skepticism.

"Less interesting ones," he said, closing the wardrobe door.

"Professor," the nurse said, "can I speak to you in private?"

"Certainly."

"Professor," she said when they were alone in the corridor, "I've been a nurse near fifteen years, and I've *never* seen a bite like that poor girl has on her neck."

"Have you ever seen a vampire's bite?" Van Helsing said, patronizingly.

"Vampire's bite, me foot! That 'bite' is a bloody hickey! And, I've seen plenty o' them!"

"A hickey!?!"

"You know," Nurse O'Herlihy said, "when a boy and a girl get a little carried away, and...."

"Yes," Van Helsing interrupted, "I get the picture."

"What's your game, Professor?"

"I beg your pardon?"

"Look, Professor," Nurse O'Herlihy said, "I'm a good Catholic Irish-woman, I am. I believe in the good Lord, the good little leprechauns, and an occasional good roll in the hay. I do *not* believe in vampires."

"Really?" Van Helsing said, indicating the occult magazine in her apron pocket, "I'd have thought differently."

"I also read *Alice in Wonderland.* That doesn't mean I believe the drivel."

"Miss Mina is a sweet girl. I won't let you hurt her."

"I can assure you, Miss O'Herlihy," Van Helsing said, "I am only helping her."

"Then what is all this…?"

"Can't we talk about this at another time?" Van Helsing lowered his voice, as two nurses passed them in the corridor.

"I'm off duty in fifteen minutes," Nurse O'Herlihy said. "My room is on the top floor…and my given name is 'Lucy.'"

She winked, and then reentered Mina's room, leaving Van Helsing to ponder this remarkable woman.

"Feel better, Albert, dear?"

Bela opened his eyes to find himself lying on a stone floor, staring up at that grotesque-looking bearded man in drag who scared the shit out of him while he was climbing up the trellis to Mina DeKooning's hospital room.

"Would you like me to rub your feet?" Renfield asked dotingly, as he cradled Bela's head with one arm while patting his forehead with a damp cloth.

Dracula shook has head.

"Hungry?" Renfield asked.

Dracula nodded, tentatively.

"Good," Renfield said, laying Bela's head gently onto the stone floor and standing up. "There's a nice juicy spider in the corner. I'll get him for you."

Dracula stared with incredulous horror, as Renfield scurried off.

How had he gotten here? He tried to remember.

He recalled crawling out from under the hospital bed after the nurse and Miss DeKooning had left the room to go on their little stroll. He'd snuck out of the room and had managed to make it down to the first floor without being seen, but then he'd spotted that orderly guarding the entrance.

Damn!

There was no other recourse but to follow the stairs down to the basement level. That place was dark and damp, except for one gas lamp next to a door at the end of the hallway. He headed for the door.

The room, also lit by a single light, had four long tables sitting in its center; the kind of tables that morticians use. When Bela saw that a body covered with a sheet occupied one of the tables, he realized that he was in the hospital's morgue.

His first instinct was to head back down the hallway from which he'd come, but then he spotted a large medical cabinet against the wall and, next to it, an exterior window and an exit door. *Escape!*

Bela summoned his courage and moved forward into the room, being careful to maintain his distance from the corpse on the table. When he reached the exit door, he'd found it padlocked. Frustrated, he shook it a couple of times, with no positive result, then headed back toward the corridor door.

As he passed the occupied table, a hand, apparently Renfield's, suddenly reached out from under the sheet, grasped his arm and *that's* when he fainted.

Bela looked around the room.

Renfield was over in the corner trying to catch that repulsive spider. Sucking blood or giving hickeys was one thing, but there was no way that Dracula was going to eat a goddamn spider.

He wasn't halfway to the corridor door when Renfield spotted him and started chasing him around the tables. "Stop this foolishness, Albert!" the madman said. "Stop it, I say!"

"I'm not Albert!" Dracula said, his voice hoarse.

"Are you insane?" Renfield said. "Of course, you're Albert! Who else would you be?"

"Anybody! But, *not* Albert!" He bolted for the corridor door, but Renfield was quicker and blocked his path.

"If you're not Albert," Renfield said, his arms folded, "then you can't escape with me."

"Escape?"

"Tonight," Renfield nodded. "I know the way."

Sir Gerald Crofton was sitting behind his desk, pondering his next move, when he glanced up to find a bulldog-faced man in a bowler hat standing in his office doorway. "Excuse me, sir," the man said. "I'm Inspector Griggs of Scotland Yard."

"Yes?"

"Would you know a Professor Abraham Van Helsing?"

"What of it?" Crofton said.

"I've been tryin' to talk to the Professor about this friend of his, Count Dracula, and…"

"Come in, Inspector," Crofton said graciously. "I'm Sir Gerald Crofton, chief of staff. Please sit down."

"Thank you, sir," the detective said, removing his hat and taking a seat.

"What is your interest in Count Dracula?" Crofton asked.

"Our initial report said that the Professor and this Dracula chap were perpetrating some sort o' swindle in some of these little European countries. Had people believing that this Dracula was a vampire." Griggs chuckled. "Can you imagine that?"

"Yes."

"Oh!" Griggs said. "Anyway, I got witnesses that can prove that Dracula is really Jack the Ripper."

"Really?" Crofton beamed. "You have witnesses?"

"A whole pub full of 'em."

"Interesting," Crofton said to the solution to his dilemma. "Please tell me more."

Fifteen minutes later, Crofton escorted Griggs out of his office and toward the hospital's front entrance.

"I like that idea," the Inspector said. "Catchin' two rats in the same trap, an' all that."

"You might even get a promotion," Crofton said.

"'Bout time, too," Griggs said. "If they'd let me in on this Ripper case from the beginning…"

"The villain would certainly be caught by now," Crofton said, holding back a cynical smile.

"Right!" Griggs said. "Did I tell you the kind of assignments they've been giving me at the Yard?"

"Yes, you did," Crofton said quickly. "Now, get some rest, Inspector, and I will see you tonight."

Griggs exited the hospital, musing to himself, "*Chief* Inspector Trevor Griggs…*Superintendent* Trevor Griggs…"

After Griggs had left, Crofton turned to the orderly who was guarding the door. "I'm suspending all hospital visiting for twenty-four hours," he said. "Lock the door. Nobody, except staff, enters or leaves without my authority."

As the orderly bolted the door, Crofton paid no mind to the tall man with the bright red hair, dressed in an Inverness-style coat, who was lingering outside of the building.

Holmwood and another orderly, Baker, had spent the past several hours searching for Renfield on the upper floors of the hospital, and now the only other place to look was the basement. Both men were exhausted and half asleep as they headed down the dark corridor toward the morgue.

"It's a great place to catch forty," Holmwood said. "Nobody'll look for us down here."

"There's no cold meat in there, is there?" Baker asked.

"Every table is empty."

"That's good, 'cause I'd hate to sleep next to a dead one."

"Least they don't snore," Holmwood said, opening the door. The men stepped inside.

"Bow to your queen!" Renfield said, as he and Dracula brought the metal trays down onto the orderlies' heads with a *Bong*.

Van Helsing buttoned up his vest, as Nurse Lucy O'Herlihy remade the bed in her small room on the hospital's top floor. The last ninety minutes had been uncanny for the professor. Lucy was a kindred spirit, the first woman he'd felt anything for since his wife had died eight years ago. He had told her everything about how he'd met Bela and how they'd been pulling off their vampire scam.

"So, you're the big vampire hunter who charges large fees for his services," Lucy had said, a sardonic tone in her voice.

"Only to those who can afford them," Van Helsing said. "To the others, I furnish my 'vampire repellant' free of charge."

"Really?"

"Not only do my little drops keep the blood suckers away, but it's extraordinary how they seem to vanquish certain forms of anemia."

Lucy finished with the bed. She came over and stood in front of her new lover, adjusting his tie. "If your friend is still in the hospital," she said, "he could be hiding in the basement. Nobody much likes to go down there, you know."

Renfield and Dracula finished binding and placing burlap sacks over the heads of the still unconscious orderlies. "Elizabeth would have had them beheaded," Renfield said.

Bela could only nod.

They heard the sound of approaching voices in the corridor. Renfield and Dracula each picked up their metal tray and positioned themselves behind the door. "Fun, isn't it?" Renfield said with a mischievous giggle.

Both men raised their trays, ready to strike as the door opened.

"No!" Bela shouted hoarsely to Renfield, as he saw Van Helsing enter the room.

"Bow to your queen!" Renfield said, starting to bring the tray down onto the professor's head.

Bela pivoted, smashing Renfield on the head with his tray. *Bong!* The madman collapsed unconscious onto the floor.

"What the bloody hell!" Van Helsing exclaimed, then seeing his partner, "Bela!"

Dracula pointed to Renfield. "He's Queen Victoria," he said.

"I've heard." Van Helsing pointed to the two bound orderlies. "Bela, what are you doing here?" he said.

"I don't know," Dracula said, tears starting to stream from his eyes. He laid his head on the professor's shoulder and continued to weep.

"That's all right, Bela," Van Helsing said, putting his arms around him. "Tell me all about it."

Dracula wiped his eyes. "The Ripper tried to get me," he said.

"What!?!"

"He chased me here...to the hospital."

"Oh, my God!" Lucy said, moving into the room. "Jack the Ripper is in this hospital?"

"What's she doing here?" Dracula said, stepping away from Van Helsing and pointing to Nurse O'Herlihy.

"She's my friend," Van Helsing said. "She's going to help us."

"She is?"

"Bela," Van Helsing said, "the police think that *you're* the Ripper."

Dracula giggled hysterically. "What!?!"

"They have witnesses."

"I'm not a murderer," Dracula said. "I'm a vampire!"

"We'll get you out of here tonight," Van Helsing said.

"Tonight!" Dracula said. "No! *Now!*"

"Bela," Van Helsing said, "you're a vampire. If you go outside, the sunlight will destroy you."

"That's right," Bela said. "I forgot. I…" He glowered at Van Helsing. "Wait! I'm not a vampire. I'm an acrobat!"

"Make up your bloody mind."

Dracula grabbed the lapels of Van Helsing's coat. "I want out of this horrid place, now!" he said.

"There are guards at every door," Lucy said.

"Tonight, Bela," Van Helsing said, gently removing his partner's hands from his lapels, "*After* I vanquish you…for the *last* time." He turned to Lucy. "No vanquish. No fee."

"Right!" Lucy said with a nod.

The professor turned back to Dracula. "She will be our witness," he said.

Dracula pondered a moment, and then pointed to the still unconscious Renfield. "He thinks we're married,"

Van Helsing smiled. "We'll arrange a divorce," he said.

The moon was full, the streets blanketed with fog when Van Helsing returned to the hospital late that night. He was dressed in a fresh suit and topcoat, carrying his walking stick and a carpetbag.

Inspector Griggs, looking like the cat that was about to pounce onto the canary, watched from behind some bushes as an orderly admitted the professor to the secured building. They were all unaware of the tall man with bright red hair, dressed in an Inverness-style coat, who was observing them from the street.

Van Helsing found Crofton in his office, talking with Seward. "Problems, Sir Gerald?" the professor inquired.

"Two of our orderlies seem to have disappeared," Seward said.

"Possibly they're tied up somewhere," Van Helsing deadpanned.

Crofton put on his topcoat, and then removed a revolver from his desk drawer.

"That won't stop Dracula," Van Helsing said.

"Perhaps," Crofton said, taking an envelope out of the same drawer. "Incidentally, Miss DeKooning's parents are due back tomorrow, so I'd better give this to you now *before* they have a chance to object." He handed Van Helsing the envelope. "I believe that is the fee we agreed upon."

Van Helsing counted the currency in the envelope. "It is, indeed," he said.

"Are you sure you don't want a firearm, Professor? Crofton said. "I have another…."

"Everything I require is in here," Van Helsing said, indicating his carpetbag.

"When would you expect Dracula to strike?" Seward asked,

"The moon is full," Van Helsing said. "Anytime between now and dawn."

"Then we should take our stations," Crofton said.

Van Helsing shook hands with Crofton and Seward. "To the eradication of evil, gentlemen."

"Sterling thought," Crofton said.

While Van Helsing headed for Mina's room, Crofton and Seward went down to the hospital's front entrance and out the door. Griggs stepped out from his hiding place, and Crofton introduced him to his colleague. "Escort the Inspector around the building to Miss DeKooning's room," he said. "Stand guard with him beneath her window."

"What's going on?" Seward asked.

"Do as I say, Seward," Crofton said. "Miss DeKooning's life may well depend on it."

"I'll try to explain, Doctor," Griggs said, taking the bewildered Seward by the arm and leading him toward the corner of the building. Crofton waited a few moments, and then reentered the hospital.

A few minutes earlier, Dracula had left Renfield and the two orderlies tied up in the hospital's morgue and, carrying a coil of rope that he'd discovered in a utility closet, had snuck up the backstairs to the third floor. The hallway was void of life, except for Lucy, who was seated in front of Mina DeKooning's room. Spotting Bela, still in his evening clothes, she motioned him to come forward. "We only have a few minutes," she said as he hurried down the hallway toward her.

"Is the girl asleep?" Dracula asked.

Lucy nodded. "I gave her a sedative," she said.

"Good," Dracula said. "I wouldn't want to frighten her." He entered the hospital room and Lucy sat back down outside the door

Down in the morgue, an extremely irked Renfield had been able to free himself from his bonds. "Damn that Albert!" he muttered to himself. "I'll fix him! Just see how he likes sleeping in another bedroom for the next six months."

He looked over at the two orderlies; both awake but still tied securely. They were making unintelligible sounds from beneath their gags.

"Oh, shut up!" he said, picking up the metal tray and giving each man a *Bong* over the head.

Lucy was still seated in front of Mina's room as Van Helsing, carrying his carpetbag and walking stick, rounded the corner from the main stairway and headed in her direction. She stood up and went to meet him. Glancing about to make sure that they were alone, they kissed, at first, quickly, then a second, more lingering meeting of the lips.

"Lucy, my love," Van Helsing said, catching his breath, " this is not the most opportune time…"

"I know." Lucy kissed him even more passionately, and then abruptly broke away. "Good evening, Professor," she said, a neutral expression on her face.

"Nurse," he said, following her straight-faced lead. "How is the patient?"

"Sleeping," Lucy said. "Her color looks so much better."

"Naturally," Van Helsing said. "What do you think I am? A charlatan?"

He discarded his topcoat and walking stick onto Lucy's chair, and then removed a large crucifix from the carpetbag. "Ready?" he said to the nurse.

"Ready," Lucy said with a wink.

"Then, let us do battle with the undead."

Lucy flung open the door. Brandishing the crucifix, Van Helsing burst into Mina's room, which was lit only by moonlight.

"Aha!" he said with a large slice of ham.

Except for the sleeping Mina, the room was empty. Van Helsing looked at Lucy. She shrugged. He surveyed the room. "Bela?" he whispered.

The wardrobe door opened. "What?" Dracula said, sticking his head out.

"Are you ready?" Van Helsing scowled.

"Sorry."

Lucy tried to keep a straight face, as Dracula moved over to the bed and raised his cape, as if to envelope Mina. He indicated that Van Helsing should continue.

The professor let out a sigh of exasperation, then again brandished the crucifix, as he and his partner began their well-rehearsed routine. "Aha!" he said with an even greater dramatic flair.

Dracula leaped back from the bedside. "Van Helsing!" he exclaimed, out hamming his partner. "We meet again!"

"For the last time, Count!"

Standing in the doorway, Lucy couldn't help but giggle to herself.

"Curses!" Dracula said. He moved toward the window.

"There is no escape through the window," Van Helsing said, improvising a warning. "My companion below is armed with a revolver."

Dracula stopped. "A revolver!?!" he said, then with a false bravado: "Bullets cannot harm me, Professor. You know that."

Van Helsing put his fingers to his lips, then moved over to the window and opened it. "Gentlemen!" he called below. "I need you!"

From the window, Van Helsing watched two shadowy figures hurry off toward the front of the hospital. He turned back toward Dracula, thus he did not see one of them stop and then return to his post below the window.

"I'll meet you back at your hotel," Van Helsing said to Bela. He handed him the envelope Crofton had given him containing the fee. "Take care of this."

Dracula looked surprised. "You trust me with this?" he said.

"You're my partner, aren't you?? Van Helsing said. "Now, go!"

Dracula reached down and grabbed the coil of rope he'd carried up from the basement. He had tied one end of the cord to a window post. He quickly climbed up onto and outside of the windowsill, and then prepared to repel himself down to the ground.

"One moment!" Sir Gerald Crofton stood in the doorway of the room, his revolver pointed at Dracula.

"Sir Gerald!" Lucy exclaimed.

"Crofton!" Van Helsing said.

Crofton cocked the weapon. "Thought you might need some help, Professor," he said.

Dracula squinted at Crofton, recognizing him. Petrified, he pointed at the man with one hand, while hanging onto the rope with the other. "The…The…The Ripper!!!" he shouted.

Van Helsing leaped forward, grabbing Crofton's arm just as he fired the revolver. The shot went wild, hitting the upper windowsill.

Dracula let go of the rope, falling out of the window.

Beneath the window, Griggs looked up in horror as a screaming Dracula plunged down toward him. He, also, managed a scream before the "vampire" landed on top of him, thereby breaking his fall and knocking the detective unconscious.

Van Helsing, Lucy and Crofton rushed to the window. They saw Dracula struggle to his feet, and then limp off into the fog. "He's getting away," Van Helsing said, relieved.

He looked over at Mina, who was still sleeping peacefully, and then turned to face Crofton. "Sir Gerald…"

The eminent physician was no longer in the room.

"Where'd he go?" Van Helsing asked.

"He was here a moment ago," Lucy said.

"What did Bela shout just before he fell?"

Lucy pondered a moment. "It sounded like… 'The Ripper.'" she said.

"The Ripper?" Van Helsing said, walking with Lucy out into the hallway. "What the bloody hell did he mean by that?"

He was repacking his carpetbag when Seward rounded the corner and hurried down the hallway toward them. "Professor," he shouted, "are you all right?"

"Of course, I'm all right," Van Helsing said. "Have you seen Sir Gerald?"

"He just left the hospital. Said he was pursuing the vampire."

"My God!" Van Helsing said. "Seward, take care of the patient." He turned to Lucy. "Nurse, come with me."

"But…" Seward looked bewildered.

"Do it, Doctor!" Van Helsing said. "The future of all England may depend on you."

"Bit much, wasn't that?" Lucy said, as she and Van Helsing hurried down the hallway toward the stairway.

"When we were in the morgue," Van Helsing said, "didn't Bela say that the Ripper had chased him to the hospital?"

"He did," Lucy said, starting to descend the stairs. "Abraham, you're not suggesting…?"

"According to the newspapers, the Ripper disembowels his victims 'with the skill of an accomplished surgeon'."

"But, Sir Gerald!?!" Lucy protested.

"If Bela knows that Crofton is, indeed, the Ripper, then Sir Gerald must dispose of him…and what easier way to do that than to vanquish a vampire?

"My God! I've given him the way."

As Van Helsing and Lucy reached the ground floor of the hospital, Griggs appeared at the foot of the stairs. He was still a bit dazed, but ready to do his duty. "Not so fast, Professor," he said.

"What do you want?" Van Helsing said.

"I hereby arrest you as an accomplice in the Jack the Ripper murders."

"You must be joking!" Van Helsing said, attempting to move past him.

Griggs took hold of Van Helsing's arm. "Hold on!" he said, turning his back to the stairway. "It'll go easier on you if you come quietly."

"Bow to your queen!"

Bong!

Van Helsing and Lucy turned to see Griggs collapse unconscious onto the floor. Renfield stood just behind him at the head of the basement stairs, holding a metal tray.

"Thank you, your Majesty," Van Helsing said, bowing slightly.

"Quite all right!" Renfield said.

As the professor and Lucy hurried toward the hospital's front entrance, Renfield looked down at Griggs. "General Gordon?" he said, somewhat surprised. "I thought you were dead."

Lucy diverted the attention of the orderly standing guard at the door while Van Helsing maneuvered past him. The professor hurried toward the street, searching for a Hansom. He did not notice the man with bright red hair, dressed in an Inverness-style coat, who was walking toward the hospital entrance.

The man recognized Van Helsing, as he rushed by him. "Professor!" he called, but the fog had already swallowed up the renowned vampire hunter.

A distraught Dracula entered his hotel room and shut the door, leaning against it exhausted.

A few moments later, he heard footsteps coming down the hallway toward him. He tensed, listened. The footsteps were drawing nearer.

He looked around for somewhere to hide. His eyes rested on the coffin-like crate that was upright against the wall. He moved across the room.

The door opened and Crofton entered, closing it behind him. The room appeared to be empty, but then the doctor noticed the coffin-sized crate. He chuckled to himself, removed the revolver from inside his coat pocket and pointed it toward the box.

He fired twice at its center, the bullets ripping through the wood.

He moved to the front of the crate, holding the revolver in one hand and flinging the top of the crate open with the other.

The receptacle was empty, except for the two exit holes that the bullets had made in the back.

Surprised, Crofton looked about for his quarry. He even ducked down to check under the bed. He moved toward the window, which was slightly ajar.

Had he opened it and looked outside, he would have seen Dracula hanging from the upper window frame, two stories above the street.

Crofton continued to search the room. He had just turned his back toward the window when, suddenly, Dracula came crashing through the glass, landing on top of him. Both men went sprawling.

"Idiot!" a dazed Dracula muttered to himself.

Crofton regained his feet first. "I beg your pardon?" he said, leveling the revolver at Dracula, who propped himself up onto his elbows.

"Not you," Dracula said. "Me! For attempting such a ridiculous thing."

"Very gallant!" Crofton said. "Too bad we must end it here, old man. The Ripper and the vampire…We'd make quite a pair."

"We could terrorize London together," Dracula suggested directly. "You would disembowel our victims, and I would drink their blood."

Crofton laughed. "Were it only possible," he said. "Unfortunately, I wish to cease my nocturnal wanderings for the time being…and, that's where you enter the picture, my friend. Inspector Griggs already believes that you're the Ripper. Perhaps we should make him a hero."

"You win!" Dracula said, holding up his hands. "I will surrender myself to Inspector Griggs."

"No," I think I'm going to have to shoot you, and then drive a stake through your heart. That *is* the way you kill a vampire, isn't it?"

"Absolutely not!" Dracula said. "Wait 'til morning. Take me out into the sunlight, and I'll crumble into dust."

Crofton produced a small wood stake and hammer from his other coat pocket. "If only we had the time," he said. He moved toward Dracula who, quite frightened, got to his feet and backed toward the coffin crate. Crofton cocked the revolver, pointed it at him.

"No!" Dracula said, covering his face.

Suddenly, the door to the room was kicked open.

Van Helsing stood silhouetted in the opening.

"Abraham!" Dracula shouted.

Crofton turned the revolver toward Van Helsing and fired. The bullet hit the doorjamb, just missing the professor's head.

In a surge of newfound fortitude, Dracula rushed Crofton, tackling him around the middle and propelling him back toward the broken window. Both men went plunging through the opening, screaming.

Van Helsing rushed to the window. "Bela!"

Lying on the street below was a single body, Crofton's.

"Bela?" Van Helsing said.

"What?"

Van Helsing looked down and saw Dracula hanging by his fingertips from the outside windowsill.

"Come in here," the professor said, grabbing Bela's arms and finding it difficult to conceal his happiness at finding his friend alive.

The Hansom cab stopped in front of Waterloo Station in late afternoon. The driver stepped down and opened the door for Nurse Lucy O'Herlihy, out of uniform and dressed in her street clothes. She paid the man, and then indicated that he should take her several pieces of luggage inside the station.

She spotted Van Helsing inside the busy depot, buying a newspaper, and hurried over to him. "I was so worried," she said.

"Everything is fine," Van Helsing said, embracing her. "Did you get my luggage?"

Lucy nodded, as they started walking toward the train platforms. "The hospital is a madhouse," she said. "The police came. Told us that Sir Gerald was killed while chasing the Ripper."

"A noble epitaph," Van Helsing said.

"Renfield's escaped again."

"What else is new?" he said with a smile. "How's Miss DeKooning?"

"Her father has returned. He's calling her progress a miracle."

"That is very good news."

"Even better," Lucy said, "Dr. Seward is now acting chief of staff. He'd like you back at the hospital…to continue your research."

"Really?" Van Helsing beamed.

"Professor!"

Van Helsing looked around to see the man with bright red hair, dressed in an Inverness-style coat, rushing through the crowd toward him.

"You!" Lucy appeared irked at the man. She turned to Van Helsing. "This clod has been annoying me with questions ever since last night."

"What the bloody hell do you want?" Van Helsing said to the man.

"Excuse me, Professor," the man said. "I'm a writer. Name is Stoker. Bram Stoker."

"Yes?"

"I've followed your exploits as a vampire hunter in the Balkan press, and I'd like to write a book about you."

"You jest."

"No!" Stoker said. "I've already spoken to a publisher, and he's willing to pay a sizable advance for your story."

"Really?" Van Helsing said, suddenly interested.

"Got you now, Professor!" Inspector Griggs slapped his large hand onto Van Helsing's shoulder. "You're under arrest!"

"On what charge?" Van Helsing carefully removed Griggs' hand from his person.

"Like I said back at the hospital," Griggs said. "Accomplice to Count Dracula, alias Jack the Ripper."

"Dracula!?!"

"Right!" Griggs said.

"Inspector," Van Helsing said, "have you been reading my notes?"

"What notes?"

Van Helsing pointed to the man with bright red hair. "The notes for the book that young Stoker and I are writing together."

"I don't know nothing 'bout no book," Griggs said.

"Count Dracula happens to be a character in our book," Van Helsing said, "and if you attempt to plagiarize it, Stoker and I will sue both you and Scotland Yard. Isn't that right, Stoker?"

"We certainly will," Stoker said.

"A character in a book?" Griggs mumbled to himself. "I'll have to talk to the Superintendent 'bout that."

Van Helsing and Lucy couldn't help but chuckle, as they watched Griggs, utterly baffled, wander off toward the exit. Stoker also joined in, even though he was not quite sure what he was laughing about.

Dracula was sitting in the private compartment he'd rented, waiting for the train to depart, when the outer door opened and Van Helsing entered from the platform. "I was getting worried that you'd miss the train," Dracula said. "Where is Miss Lucy?"

"Bela, my partner, my friend," Van Helsing said, sitting next to him, "the game is over."

"Over?"

"I'm afraid the wolves are closing in. There are not many places where we can safely present our little charade any longer."

"But, what will we do?"

"You will take the large amount of money in your breast pocket," Van Helsing said. "Travel the Continent, and live like an aristocrat. Or, perhaps you'd like to form your own circus?"

"I will live like an aristocrat," Dracula said. "But, what about you?"

"I have the bank account in Vienna, and some opportunities have presented themselves here in London that I wish to explore."

The two men stared at each other for a long moment, and then Van Helsing stood up, as did Dracula. "I shall miss your…lunacy," Van Helsing said.

"I shall miss your foul temper."

They grasped, shook hands, warmly, both men fighting the emotion inside of them. "Perhaps we shall meet again in Transylvania," Dracula said.

"Perhaps." Van Helsing looked, once again, into his friend's eyes, and then exited the compartment.

He stood on the platform as the train pulled out. After it had disappeared from sight, he walked back into the station, joining Lucy and Stoker at the refreshment stand. He kissed Lucy on the check, and then turned to the man with the bright red hair. "Well, young man," he said, "shall we write the kind of book that legends spring from?"

Dracula smiled as he counted the extraordinarily large amount of currency in the envelope Van Helsing had given him. He put the money back into his jacket and rang for the porter.

"Yes, sir?" the elderly man said, as he slid back the compartment door.

"Caviar and champagne," Dracula ordered.

"Very good, sir." He shut the door behind him.

Dracula picked up the newspaper Van Helsing had left and began to read. A few moments later, there was a knock at the door.

"Enter," Dracula said. He heard the door slide open and then shut. When he glanced up, his mouth dropped open. He blanched.

Renfield, still dressed in his matronly outfit, stood in front of him, hands on his hips. "Albert," the madman said, "do you know the trouble you've caused me? This infantile behavior has got to stop!"

○

Big Al and Desperate Dan

There was this story about Big Al floating around after the War.

That's Al Capone to you.

I was in the middle of a five-year stretch at Joliet when it happened, but a couple of guys I met a few years later, when I was a resident of Sing Sing, swear the story is true.

Big Al was only forty when they released him from Lewisberg in 1939, but somewhere along the line he'd picked up "a nail," and his health was not good. They say, he looked like he was sixty. He'd lost weight and his mind wasn't right either.

Things had changed since 1931 when the Feds sent Al away on that tax rap. He used to be King of Chicago. Now, there was a national syndicate and Jake Guzik was running the Chicago operation. He'd sent word to Al that he should "retire" to Florida and the boys would guarantee that he would live out his days "like a king." Chicago, they said, was off-limits.

That didn't sit too well with Big Al. "Chicago is *my* town," he said. "I *am* Chicago."

But, after he saw some doctors in Baltimore, Al went to Florida. He used the moniker "Al Brown" there. Figured it would make him more anonymous. He didn't want the neighbors to be scared of him.

Actually, those rich neighbors weren't scared at all. They knew who Big Al was, and they got a kick out of the fact that they were living next to America's most famous mobster.

Al stayed at that big estate of his for the next year or so, walking through all the rooms ten times a day, shouting at his guys, shouting at the walls, shouting at Hymie Weiss, who was long dead.

Al had seen to that.

Then, he'd sit in a chair and just stare out the window for hours. Wouldn't say a word.

Al may have been going nuts, but he also had a plan, and in the late fall of 1941, he put that plan into action.

One day, Vince Lupo, a guy who did jobs for Al, shows up at the house with this other fella. This guy, his name was John Dalton, didn't look too happy about being there. He was average height, probably in his late thirties. He talked like he came off the farm and he was dressed in a suit that was seven years out of style. A real rube.

Larry Volpe greeted them at the door. Larry was in his mid-forties, a six-foot tall former boxer. When Larry spoke, he was speaking for Big Al.

"Mr. Dalton," Larry said, "I'm Larry Volpe."

"Why am I here?" John Dalton asked. They shook hands.

"The man I work for has a proposition for you."

"And who's that?"

"Mr. Brown," Larry said.

"He sure went to a hell of a lot of trouble to get me here."

"Sorry if our boys were a little rough," Larry said, "but he wasn't sure you'd come."

"They didn't ask," John Dalton said.

Larry took this Dalton fellow into the study, and then told Edward, the butler, to get them some beers.

Big Al always liked having a butler. He figured it gave him "class," even if he did call the guy "Eddie."

A few minutes later, Al walked into the room, wearing white silk pajamas under a white-striped maroon dressing gown. They say that, even though his movements were a bit jerky and he walked with a cane, he was still his old outgoing self. "I'm Al Brown," he said to John Dalton.

"No, you're not," John Dalton said. "You're Capone...Al Capone."

Al laughed and turned to Larry. "I heard he was a smart fella," he said.

"I read the papers," John Dalton said.

"I haven't been in them much, lately," Al said. He lit up a Havana. "But that'll change."

They sat down on the sofa, and then Al told Larry to have the cook scramble them some eggs.

"Why am I here, Mr. Capone?" John Dalton asked.

"I'm 'Al' to my friends."

"*Why* am I here?"

Al sucked on his Havana. "Understand you ran with Dillinger," he said.

John Dalton nodded. "I did a couple of jobs with him."

"Guess you got out before things got too hot."

"Yeah, I did."

"Smart."

The two of them just sat there for nearly a full minute. Nobody said a word. They say you could hear a dog fart.

"Where is he?" Al said, finally.

"Where's who?"

"Dillinger."

"He's dead," John Dalton said. "You know that." He looked at Al like he was totally nuts. A couple of the guys looked at the Boss like he was nuts, too.

"The Feds killed him in Chicago in 1934," Dalton continued. "He was coming out of the Biograph Theater."

Al shook his head and chuckled. "Now, we both know that that's not true, don't we?"

Big Al hardly gave Dalton or the other guys in the room a minute to think about that before he was up on his feet, pacing the room. "I used to love hangin' around the Brooklyn Navy Yards," he said, "watching them work that big crane they had there."

Dalton seemed bewildered. The guys seemed bewildered.

"And, when they changed the Marine guard," Al cackled, "I mean, these guys walked so stiff you'd of thought they had broomsticks up their asses."

"Those Marines are pretty tough hombres," Dalton said. "I remember when I was in the Navy...."

"You were in the Navy?" Al interrupted.

"Yeah..."

"So was Dillinger," Al said. "Is that where you met 'im?"

"No..." John Dalton said, "That was later."

Big Al smiled. "Hey," he said, "did you know that Dillinger and me had the same mouthpiece?"

"No," John Dalton said. "I didn't know that."

"Yeah, he's the one that told me," Big Al said. "That whole thing was a set-up, and this shmuck, Jimmy Lawrence, was the patsy."

"Lawrence?"

"Yeah," Big Al said, "he's the guy that the Feds shot in front of the Biograph."

"That's a pretty good story."

Big Al cackled again. "It gets better," he said. "A couple days later, the Feds found out for sure that they'd blasted the wrong man. This was *after* all those fantastic news stories. You know, 'FBI Kills Dillinger' on every front page in the country."

"I saw 'em," John Dalton said.

"It was embarrassin'," Big Al said with glee. "Ol' J. Edgar Hoover told his henchmen that such a 'revelation' could destroy the FBI. He was afraid that we'd all see him for the dumb bastard that he is."

Big Al sucked some more on his cigar. "Anyway," he said, "they hushed it up. They deported that Anna Sage dame.

"You know, the 'Lady in Red,' to keep her quiet, an' they sent word to Dillinger through the shyster that if he'd 'retire,' they'd leave him alone."

Big Al plopped down onto the sofa next to John Dalton and laughed. He continued to laugh until his guys, who didn't really understand what was so funny, figured that they'd better start laughing, too.

John Dalton didn't laugh.

"Hey," Big Al said, trying to enlighten him, "it'd sure look funny if the FBI killed him twice, wouldn't it?"

John Dalton was deadpan. "I guess it would," he said. "But, John Dillinger is dead."

"You don't look very dead to me, John," Big Al said.

John Dalton, they say, turned white as a sheet.

Big Al laughed again, slapped him on the shoulder. "Do you really think I'd go to all this trouble to send my boys up to Oregon or Washington, or whatever damn boondocks state you're hidin' out in, to bring me back some pissy little bank robber named John Dalton?"

"Your boys brought you the wrong man," John Dalton said.

Big Al turned to Lupo. "You bring me the wrong man, Vince?"

"Nope," Lupo said. "That's John Dalton from Walla Walla, Washington. Grabbed him comin' out of the barber shop."

Big Al turned back to John Dalton and grinned. "Don't they know how to give a decent haircut in Walla Walla?"

"Guess not," John Dalton said.

"Dillinger," Big Al said, "the sooner you stop playing footsie with me, the sooner I can make you a very rich man."

John Dalton didn't say a word.

"You want to think about it?" Big Al said. "That's fine. Let's go have those eggs."

Big Al didn't wait for an answer. He walked out of the study, heading for the formal dining room with Lupo and his other guys following.

Only Larry Volpe lingered behind. He waited until Big Al and the guys were out of earshot before he turned to John Dalton. "Look, fella," he said, "I don't know if you're John Dillinger, or John Dalton, or Popeye, the Sailor Man. And, frankly, I don't really give a goddamn.

"But, if you want to get out of here in one piece, you'd better be Dillinger. Kapish?"

John Dalton nodded. "What's wrong with him?" he asked.

"What do you mean?"

Dalton gestured, as if to say, "You know what I mean."

Volpe shrugged. "Al hasn't been 'right' since he got out of the joint."

"What do the doctors say?"

"They can't do much, 'cause Al doesn't like needles," Volpe said. "He's still Al Capone. You don't argue with him."

"I'd like to call my family," Dalton said. "Let them know I'm okay."

"Sure," Volpe said. "Use the phone on Al's desk."

Dalton walked over to the large ornate oak desk that sat in front of the room's bay window and picked up the phone receiver.

"Just be careful what you say," Volpe said.

Dalton made his phone call, and then Volpe walked him into the dining room where Big Al was stuffing an over-easy egg into his mouth. The yolk was dripping onto his chin.

"Hey, there you are," Big Al said to Dalton. "Mike," he said to one of his guys, "get our guest some ham and eggs."

While Mike filled a plate for him from the buffet, Dalton sat down at the table.

"My cook makes the best eggs you ever tasted," Big Al said with his mouth full.

"Good," John Dalton said. "I'm hungry."

Big Al wiped his mouth with the back of his hand. "So," he said, "ready to talk some business?"

John Dalton nodded.

"You know, them first years I was 'away,' I kept hearing about you," Big Al said. "Word'd come into the cellblocks about this gutsy young hood that'd go with his gang into bank after bank... He'd smile at the teller, draw his rod, then he'd leap over the counter..."

"Those were my 'Desperate Dan' days," John Dalton said.

"Huh?"

"The papers didn't know who I was then, so they tagged me 'Desperate Dan.'" Dalton said with a chuckle. "I guess I'd seen too many Doug Fairbanks movies."

Big Al lowered his voice. "Well," he said, "that's what I need now, a Douglas Fairbanks. Or, at least, a John Dillinger."

He glanced over at Lupo, who was leaning against the door arch, picking his nose. "Hey," he snapped, "get me an umbrella while you're up there."

Lupo's reaction was blank.

"We're eatin' here," Big Al said. "You got nuthin' better to do?"

Lupo shrank back out of the room.

"These young goons," Big Al said to Dalton, "they're not like the guys in the old days. They're loyal alright, but you can't trust 'em."

"Okay, Al," John Dalton said. "What do you have in mind?"

"I want you to go to Chicago for me."

"I don't think so."

"Why not?"

"Too many people know me there."

"Who's going to notice?" Big Al said. "You're dead."

John Dalton shook his head. "Yeah, but..."

"You had your face changed, didn't you?"

John Dalton nodded.

"Then don't worry about it," Big Al said. "I guarantee nobody'll recognize you.

"I got bucks stashed in Chi. Over fifteen million in cash. You go up there and bring it back to me."

"Why don't you go get it?" John Dalton asked.

"People're watchin' me."

"Who?"

"The Feds, for one."

"Who else?"

Big Al, as he was prone to do, suddenly turned angry. "A bunch of assholes that used to work for me," he said. "While I was in stir, they pushed me out. I built the goddamn organization, and they 'retired' me to a life of 'Florida comfort'."

He stood up from the table and held his cane up like a baseball bat. "There were a couple of guys who tried to screw with me once," he said. "I held a banquet in their honor, and then I played baseball with their goddamn heads."

He smashed the cane down onto the table. John Dalton jumped in his chair.

"I get my hands on my fifteen mil," Big Al said, "and I'm going to buy back my town. Then, I'm gonna play a lot more baseball…

"Hey," Big Al said with a smile, "you wanna see my swimmin' pool?"

"Sure."

Big Al turned to Mike. "Tell Eddie to bring us some coffee."

Ambling along with his cane, Big Al led John Dalton out through the French doors into the back yard and down four steps to the large rectangular swimming pool. Volpe and Mike stayed at the top of the steps. Al plopped down onto a chaise lounge and Dalton took the chair next to him.

"Five months it took my boys to track you down," Big Al said. "What's a guy like you doin' farmin' in the toolies??"

"I don't know," John Dalton said. "Maybe I wanted a simpler life; a family."

"A family's great," Big Al said. "Mine's away right now visitin'. But that ain't for *you*. A guy like you would find that boring."

"Hiding out and getting shot at can be pretty boring, too."

John Dalton stopped talking. Edward was there with the coffee.

"Will there be anything else, sir?" the butler asked.

"Naw," Big Al said. "That's it, Eddie… Blow."

Eddie blew.

John Dalton took a sip from his fancy china cup. "I think I started wantin' out when 'Red' Hamilton got his," he said. "A slug in the back from some dumb deputy…We buried poor Red in a goddamn gravel pit. I had to pour lye over his face first so's nobody'd recognize him.

"So, I ask myself, 'Johnny, do you wanna wind up like that? Or, maybe you wanna join ol' Harry Pierpont in the death house?'

"It was time for a change."

"How'd you pull it off?" Big Al asked.

"It weren't too hard," John Dalton said. He took a gulp from his fancy china cup.

"Come on," Big Al said, "tell me how you did it."

John Dalton smiled. "You're a nosey son-of-a-bitch," he said.

"Okay, while I was doin' the plastic surgery stuff, an acquaintance found this Jimmy Lawrence guy up in Wisconsin someplace. He was a small-time pimp. Looked somethin' like me…We paid 'im to hang around Chi, make some noises like he *was* me while I covered my tracks… I guess he played the part *too* good.

"Those Feds are real trigger-happy, ain't they?"

"Don't expect me to defend them," Big Al said.

"Anyway, I wound up on the west coast…met my wife…She's a good lady…

"But, I knew somebody'd show up one day."

"You're lucky it was my guys," Big Al said.

John Dalton filled his fancy china coffee cup again. "When I was a kid," he said, "I wanted to be Jesse James. I read everything 'bout him I could lay my hands on. I loved the way he stuck it to the railroads, the banks. Then, he'd turn around and help out some poor old widow lady who was gonna lose her farm.

"Me? I'd get my hands on the bank's dough, spend it on booze, women and say, 'screw the widow lady'."

"John," Big Al said, "you were just too small time."

John Dalton looked like he'd been slapped in the face. "What?" he said.

"Don't get me wrong," Big Al said.

"You're telling me that *I* was small time?"

"Oh, you were front page news alright," Big Al said. "Just like Jesse James. Bigger even."

"Damn right I was!" John Dalton said. "Hell, I used to call up the goddamn Feds on the phone and *dare* 'em to catch me."

"You made good news copy," Big Al said. "Folks were rootin' for you…because you were an outsider."

"That's right."

"But, outsiders never win. You were gettin' shot at, workin' for nickels and dimes."

"I did okay," John Dalton said.

"What'd you clear each job? Two or three grand per man? That's hamburger money where I come from.

"Me? I was big business."

John Dalton looked like he was getting angry. "Outsiders never win, huh?" he muttered. "At least, I never went around havin' people killed."

"Hey!" Big Al said. "I was convicted of not payin' my taxes. Nothin' else."

John Dalton glowered at Big Al.

Big Al glowered back.

Standing at the top of the steps, Mike and Larry Volpe weren't sure if the two of them were about to attack each other.

"John," Big Al said after a minute or so, "I need a guy with your balls to go up to Chi for me. I'm offerin' you more money than you'd clear if you robbed every bank in the fuckin' Midwest. You can take yer family, retire in South America and live like a goddamn king."

"How much?" John Dalton said.

"A ten thousand guarantee against ten percent of whatever you bring back. Bring back the whole bundle an' that comes to a million and a half."

"Sounds like there could be some opposition."

"Small potatoes," Big Al said. "You can handle it."

"You're full of shit, Capone."

"I know that."

"But, I like you."

"I like you, too," Big Al said.

"I don't *trust* you."

"You don't have to," Big Al said. "So, what do you say?"

"I could use some action."

"Good!"

"It's gonna cost you *twenty* percent, though" John Dalton said.

Big Al laughed. "John," he said, "you got me over a barrel. You want twenty percent? You got fifteen."

"Where you got the dough stashed?"

"You know the Lexington Hotel?

"On Michigan?"

"I got a hidden vault there," Big Al said.

"That's eight years ago," John Dalton said. "Somebody might've found it by now."

"I'd've heard."

"I'll take the train up to Chicago," John Dalton said. "Look the place over."

"Take my Caddy," Big Al said. "I know you got a new pan and yer 'dead,' but why take a chance that you run into an ol' friend on the train?"

"Okay."

"Yer gonna need help, so I'm sending Larry along with you."

"I like to pick my own gang," John Dalton said.

"Don't worry about it," Big Al said. "Larry'll follow your directions, just like they were mine.

"Besides, you need Larry. He knows the Lex, where the vault is, how to get into it. And, most important, how to get out of the joint without anyone knowin'."

"If he knows all that, why not let him do the job? What do ya need me for?"

"They know Larry at the Lex," Big Al said. "And, if somethin' went wrong...."

"He's a smart fella, but he don't think that fast. I need someone creative like you.

"Don't worry. You can trust him. He's the only one 'cept me who knows who you really are."

Next morning, Larry and this John Dalton guy drive off in the Caddy, headin' for Chi. Four or five days go by, and there's not a word from them.

Big Al's goin' real nuts, now. He's smashin' stuff with his cane. He's shouting at Hymie Weiss. He's even lookin' in the closets, thinkin' that Weiss is hiding in one of 'em.

"Weiss is dead," the guys tell 'im, but Big Al don't listen.

Then, one night, Big Al's playin' gin with Lupo, and he's not a happy man. Lupo's winning, and that ain't a good idea. It ain't a healthy idea either.

The phone rings. It's Larry Volpe. This Dalton guy's got a plan. They're gonna empty the vault the next night.

Big Al looks happy as a clam, and then he says to Larry, "Just be sure you take care of our friend."

Larry must've objected to that, because Big Al suddenly turned angry and said, "He's already a dead man. You can't kill him twice."

Then, he hung up.

Another two days go by. No word from Larry. No word from nobody.

Big Al is climbin' the walls. He's explodin' all over the place, smashin' even more stuff with his cane, glasses, whiskey bottles. He even smashed the glass cabinet where his wife kept her crystal stuff. Good thing she was away.

Finally, Lupo makes a couple calls to guys he knows in Chi.

Turns out there'd been some gunplay at the Lex a night or two before. Nobody knows who got shot or who did the shooting, and if they *did* know, nobody's talkin'.

By this time, Big Al's packin' his .38, and every time he thinks he sees Weiss, which is a couple times a day, he shoots it off. There're holes in the ceiling, in the French doors. Lupo, Mike and the other guys are just trying to stay out of his way.

Then, about a week later, they find Larry's body floating in Lake Michigan. He had two slugs in him.

"Where's my dough?" Big Al wants to know. "Where's Dillinger?"

Now, the guys know that Big Al is totally off his rocker. After all, everybody knew that the Feds killed Dillinger in 1934.

Lupo, he takes the train up to Chi to see what he can find out, but there's no trace of that John Dalton guy and nobody knows nothin' about any vault or any money.

Al tells Lupo to head back to Walla Walla, but when he gets there, Dalton and his family are gone. The local rubes tell 'im that Dalton's wife just disappeared one day, after she got a long distance phone call. Nobody knew where she went.

I figure that she and Dalton must've had some sort of escape plan in place. When he called her from Big Al's place, that was her cue to get lost.

And, that's about it.

A few weeks later, Pearl Harbor got bombed, and everybody sort of forgot about John Dalton or John Dillinger or whoever the guy was, and started thinkin' about Germans and Japs.

Big Al never got any better. He just got worse. Hymie Weiss was always chasin' him.

Al, finally, croaked in 1947. You know, he was just 48 years old.

In 1985, this TV show announced that they'd discovered Big Al's secret vault in the basement of the Lex, but when they opened it, the vault was empty. There wasn't even a nickel in there. Somebody, maybe John Dalton, had beat 'em to it.

I know what you're wonderin'.

What ever became of John Dalton, and was he *really* John Dillinger?

The truth is that I got no idea.

Your guess is as good as mine.

But, if that *was* Dillinger, then I want to find him…if he's still alive.

The cops grabbed me right after we pulled our last job together, before we split the take. And, two months later, while I'm sittin' in the cooler waitin' for trial, I hear the Feds shot him in Chicago.

So, Johnnie, if you're readin' this…

I want my dough!

○

Napoleon Brandy

The first time I laid eyes on Napoleon Bonaparte, he was stark naked.

The last time I saw him, he was about to start a world war by way of a nuclear missile.

I should explain.

Should I start with the "stark naked" part or the "nuclear missile" part?

Perhaps I should first tell you about me.

My name is Tom Bullock. I'm a 30-year-old physicist, a junior associate professor at Bayou State University.

My colleagues in the Physics Department, particularly Professor Raymond Steele-Shaw, think that I'm a screwball…just because I've invented a time transmitter.

Frankly, I think he's jealous. I mean, wouldn't you be, too, if some "kid," fifteen years your junior, came up with such a revolutionary device?

I know it sounds crazy, but I really can travel through time.

My transmitter, it's not like that huge contraption that you saw in those movie versions of H.G. Wells' *The Time Machine*.

No, my device is about the size of your cell phone. You just punch in a date, plus the latitude and longitude of where and when you want to visit, and it takes you there…before you can say "Jack Robinson" (*whoever he was*).

It's a very simple process. My device emits an electromagnetic field that creates a wormhole that allows you, and anything or anyone within two feet of you, to travel along the space/time fold.

In a way, it's like *Star Trek*, but instead of "Scotty" beaming you *up*, you get beamed backward or forward in time.

Really, I'm a genius. Albert Einstein should eat his heart out.

I admit that the first time I tried out my transmitter there were problems. I *did* short out every electrical circuit on campus.

The second time?

Not only did I take out the back-up generators, too, but for the next week, every time I'd walk through my kitchen, the Cuisinart would go on.

But, number three was the charm. I went back in time. *Way back…* to April 14, 1865.

I was in Washington, D.C. at Ford's Theater on the very night that President Abraham Lincoln was assassinated.

I materialized on stage just as John Wilkes Booth fired the fatal shot. He jumped out of the President's box right onto the stage next to me, and shouted, *"Sic semper tyrannis!"*

And, that's when I snapped his picture with my old Nikon.

That was my mistake!

When my flash went off, the actors and everybody in the audience stopped looking at Booth, limping off the stage. They all looked directly at me.

"He shot Mr. Lincoln!" somebody yelled, pointing in my direction.

"No," one of the actors on stage said (*God Bless him!*), "Booth shot him!"

"How could Booth do it?" the first guy shouted back. "He's just an actor."

Then, everybody in the audience went crazy. Men leaped out of their seats and started for the stage.

"Get him!"

"Lynch him!"

I snapped their picture, and then started backing toward the wings. "Wait!" I tried to explain. "I'm not even here."

They weren't listening. I turned and ran. I bumped into one of the actors and a stagehand, but I made it out of the back door into the alley. I punched the coordinates into my transmitter and I was gone. If the mob that was chasing me saw anything, it was just a bright yellow glow as I dematerialized.

I was back in the present day in my own physics lab, and I had done it. I had traveled back into the past and returned unharmed.

And, even better, I had absolute proof that I had done it: photographs taken in Ford's Theater on the night of April 14, 1865.

That was my other mistake.

I should have brought a *digital* camera.

The pictures didn't come out. The transmitter's electromagnetic field must've fogged the film.

Next morning, I had a meeting with the dean of the department and Professor Steele-Shaw.

Dean Whitaker seemed to be sympathetic to my plight. "Mr. Bullock," he said, "you're one of the most brilliant young physicists I've ever met. The Department has given you plenty of leeway to prove your time travel theory. But, wouldn't it be better if you concentrated your efforts on more 'practical' projects?"

"Like how to take a picture," Steele-Shaw quipped.

"Don't you understand?" I pleaded. "I did it!"

"Tom…Tommy," Whitaker said, "Time travel is impossible. Every scientist knows that."

"Maybe," Steele-Shaw said, "you fell asleep in your lab and dreamt it."

"I was *not* asleep!"

"There's a simple solution to this," Whitaker said. "If your - what do you call it? - time transmitter…works, give us a demonstration."

"I will," I said. "And, this time, I'll bring a digital camera."

"One thing I don't get, Bullock," Steele-Shaw said. "If this gadget of yours *does* work, why the past? Why not go into the future? See what's ahead of us…like who wins next year's World Series or the Kentucky Derby? You could clean up."

"The future doesn't exist yet," I said.

"So, what are you trying to accomplish?" Steele-Shaw asked. "Change history? Why didn't you warn Lincoln?"

"I don't want to change history. The ramifications on the present would be disastrous."

"So, you went back to Ford's Theater just to see the play?" Steele-Shaw said.

"I wanted to meet Abraham Lincoln, talk to him," I said. "But, my adjustments were off and I got there too late."

"Apparently."

"Professor, wouldn't it be wonderful if we could go back and meet the great men and women of history? We could bring a video camera, record them and learn from their wisdom."

Steele-Shaw's tone was sarcastic. "Fantastic idea," he said. " 'Well, Mr. Lincoln, what do you think of the play so far?' *Bang!*"

"Raymond," Whitaker interjected, "show Mr. Bullock some respect."

"Just think," I said, "what we could learn from Jefferson…Socrates… Napoleon…"

"Napoleon!" Steele-Shaw laughed. "Why not Attila the Hun?"

"Him, too!" I said. "But Napoleon was a political genius. I've read half a dozen books about him. Did you know that he devised the Napoleonic Code, the basic foundation of how governments are run today?"

"Mr. Bullock," Dean Whitaker said, perusing his desk calendar, "would it be convenient to do your demonstration this afternoon at four?"

"Yes, sir," I said. "I just need to borrow a digital camera."

"Fine, we'll do it at the football stadium. It should be empty today, and it's far enough away from the main campus that, should something go wrong, the central electrical system won't be affected."

"Good," Steele-Shaw said. "I'll clear my schedule." He headed for the door, and then turned back to face me. "Bullock," he said, "when you do your demonstration, why not go back and talk to Napoleon. Tell him his Code isn't working."

"Maybe I will," I said.

"Why *not* Napoleon," I thought to myself, as I hurried back to my lab. "He may have been a dictator, but I'll bet he was really a very nice guy."

A couple of students in the English Department had requested that, if my transmitter *did* work, they would appreciate it if I would go back to the 8th century and find somebody who could explain *Beowulf* to them…but, that trip was going to come later.

I was going to give that asshole Steele-Shaw "the finger". I was going back to June 18, 1815, and the battle of Waterloo.

I made a minor adjustment to my transmitter, grabbed a history book—so that I could prove to Napoleon or anybody else I met in 1815 that I *did* come from the future—and then I borrowed a digital camera from Rebecca.

Rebecca Kaplan is a graduate student in my department. She's a bright girl; possibly the only person on campus who doesn't think my time travel theories are "screwball".

She's cute, too. Red hair. Banjo blue eyes…

After that, I headed over to the vacant football stadium.

"You're going to Waterloo?" Dean Whitaker said, a rather disbelieving expression on his face.

"Yes, sir," I said. "I took Professor Steele-Shaw's suggestion."

"It's your show, Mr. Bullock," Dean Whitaker said. "But, I suggest, for safety's sake, you do it out in the middle of the field."

"Certainly," I said, heading out into field. "You'd better not get too close. Anything within two feet of me that's not nailed down goes along for the ride."

"Hey, Bullock," Steele-Shaw called. "When you see Napoleon, ask him why his hand is always inside his coat."

As I turned on the transmitter and it started to hum, I could hear Dean Whitaker say to Steele-Shaw, "Raymond, I think the boy is ill."

"I think he's crazy as a loon," Steele-Shaw said.

And then, suddenly, I was no longer in the football stadium.

I was standing on a muddy plain, right in the middle of the Waterloo battlefield.

Actually, I wasn't in the middle of the battlefield.

I was standing just underneath a row of French cannons, and just as I materialized, the first one fired, followed seconds later by the next one, and then every cannon down the line.

If you think Heavy Metal concerts are deafening, try standing underneath a line of cannons when they go off.

I grabbed my ears, which were ringing like Christmas bells, and then I stumbled down a short embankment, winding up in a sitting position.

Two French soldiers rushed down the hill and grabbed me by both arms. I guess they thought I was a British spy, but with "The Bells of St. Mary's" clanging in my ears, I couldn't hear a word they were saying.

They dragged me up the hill and, with their artillery captain leading them, hustled me over to a large tent. And, *that's* when I met him.

Napoleon Bonaparte, looking all of his fifty years, was sitting in an oversized metal bathtub, playing with two small wooden boats. One of the toy boats had a French flag on it and the other was adorned with a British one. He was maneuvering the boats about in his bathwater.

Kneeling behind the tub, washing his back, was a gigantic fellow with a bushy mustache. He was, as I soon learned, Napoleon's personal valet and bodyguard. His name was Gaspar.

Three high-ranking French officers were standing behind them at the other side of the tent, studying a map on a large planning table. I recognized one of them from portraits I'd seen. He was Field Marshal Michel Ney.

Napoleon, suddenly, slapped the toy British boat down with his hand, sinking it and splashing water into Gaspar's face. "*Kpow!*" he shouted, then turning to his officers: "See! *I* should have been at Trafalgar."

Ney's tone was placating. "Granted, General," he said, "but today, *now* we must deal with Wellington."

"Wellington," Napoleon scoffed, "that dimwit."

"That 'dimwit' has us vastly outnumbered," Ney countered.

Without warning, Napoleon began to sing an Italian opera in an off-key falsetto voice that, along with the ringing bells in my head, *really* gave me a splitting headache.

Gaspar spotted the two soldiers and me standing at the tent entrance. After conferring with their captain, he turned to his boss. "Sir, they've captured a spy."

Napoleon stopped singing. Everybody in the tent, particularly me, breathed a sigh of relief.

"If Wellington had us vastly outnumbered," Napoleon said to Ney, "he wouldn't be sending a spy, would he?"

"We found him hiding beneath the cannons," the captain said.

"Sabotage, ay?" Napoleon said. "Gaspar, hand me my robe."

He stood up in the tub, and there he was: naked as the day he was born.

"I see you are admiring my penis," he said as I stared at him, my mouth agape.

"No," I said, blushing.

"It is a great penis, is it not?"

I must admit that, for such a short man, he did have a damn big penis, but that's not why I was speechless. I was in the presence of Napoleon Bonaparte…and he was nude.

"A great man has a great penis," he continued, donning his purple robe. "Caesar had a great penis. Alexander the Great had a great penis…

"Gaspar here is my good, loyal servant. But, he is an ordinary man. He has an ordinary penis.

"Gaspar, show him your penis."

Gaspar rolled his eyes, as if to say, "not again," then started to undo his britches.

I had no desire to see Gaspar's penis. "That's really okay," I said.

"Whatever," Napoleon said, waving his valet away, then: "Your Wellington, he has a tiny little penis."

"He's not *my* Wellington," I said. "I don't even know the man and I've certainly never seen his penis."

"My foolish young fellow," he said. "I am Napoleon, and if I say you are a British spy…you are a British spy."

"But, I'm from Louisiana."

Napoleon turned red in the face. "*Louisiana!!!*" he shouted, turning to the captain. "Shoot him!"

"*Shoot me!?!*"

"That's what I said," he replied. "My God! Even your clothes are out of fashion." Then, to the captain: "Shoot his tailor, too."

"Right away, your Excellency," the captain said, handing Napoleon my time transmitter, digital camera and history book. "He had these things with him."

"Good work, captain." Napoleon said.

"*Wait!*" I yelled, as they dragged me out of the tent. "I'm from the future. I'm a junior associate college professor."

I kept protesting, as they dragged me toward a nearby tree. I swore that I was not British. That I'd never even been to London. That I even hated British movies because, half the time, I couldn't understand what the actors were saying.

Then, I realized that that was a dumb thing to say, because movies hadn't been invented yet.

"I don't even eat fish'n chips," I said, as they tied me to the tree. "It's deep fried…"

"You wish a last smoke?" the captain said, offering me a cigar.

"Hell, no!" I said. "You think I want to get cancer?"

The captain shrugged, and then rejoined his men, who had lined up to form a firing squad.

"I was a big fan of Brigette Bardot," I shouted, but then I realized that they wouldn't know her either.

"Ready!" the captain said to his men.

"I love French bread," I said, my voice weakening.

"Aim!"

"Bouillabaisse?"

I closed my eyes, waiting for the final command. "French fries…?"

"Wait!"

I opened my eyes to see Gaspar rushing out of Napoleon's tent and over to the captain. "His Excellency wishes to interrogate him further," I heard him say.

As I was led back to Napoleon's tent, I could hear him shouting, "Charles de Gaulle! Who the hell is Charles de Gaulle?"

I went inside, escorted by Gaspar and the captain, to find Napoleon, now dressed in his general's uniform, thumbing through my history book. "Interesting," he said, turning to me. "What's a nuclear missile?"

"It's…It's a giant, very destructive bomb," I said. "It can travel half-way across the globe."

"It can?"

"Yes, sir, your Majesty, sir."

He flipped back the pages of the book, pointing to the copyright page. "This book," he said, "it says it was published in 1997."

"I know. It's an old edition."

"It says that Wellington…with the little penis…will defeat me here at Waterloo?"

"I know," I said, trying hard to swallow.

"I will be exiled to St. Helena…where I will die?"

I could only manage a nod.

"I don't mind the dying part," he said, *"but at St. Helena!!"*

He fumed for a moment, then: "It's also a terrible portrait of me in the book. Doesn't even look like me."

"Actually," I said, "it's Marlon Brando. He played you in a movie."

"Who!?! What!?!"

Thankfully, he didn't give me an opportunity to explain that one.

"Who are you?" he demanded, "and where did you get this book?"

"My name is Tom Bullock, sir, your Majesty, and I brought this book with me from the year 2011."

Gaspar and Ney chuckled, but a stern glance from Napoleon quickly silenced them.

"How is that possible?" Napoleon asked.

I pointed to my time transmitter and digital camera that were sitting on the planning table. "May I?"

Napoleon stood aside, allowing me to retrieve them.

"This is my time transmitter," I explained. "I invented it. It allows me to visit any time and place in history."

"My word!" Napoleon said, moving to my side. "How does it work?"

"I just punch in the date, latitude and longitude of the place I want to visit, and within seconds, I'm there. " I handed him the device. "Of course, you have to know the access code."

Napoleon pondered a moment. "You mean, you could return to your own time and come back here again?"

"Sir," Ney said, "you don't believe this ridiculous..."

"Ney," Napoleon interrupted, "to avoid St. Helena, I'm willing to consider all possibilities."

"Yes, but..."

"You'd better hope this thing works," Napoleon said to his field marshal. "According to that book, you've got a date with the firing squad."

That seemed to shut Ney up.

Napoleon pointed to my camera. "And, what's this?"

"It's a digital camera, sir."

"Camera?"

"It...It makes instant portraits."

"Really!" he said, sticking his hand inside his coat per his famous pose. "You mean, I wouldn't have to sit still for hours just picking at the button in my belly?"

"May I show you?" I raised the camera to snap his picture.

"General, sir," the captain said, stepping forward, "that could be a weapon!"

"No…no," I said. Outside, I could hear the cannons firing away.

Napoleon pointed to the captain. "Make a portrait of him," he ordered.

Before the captain could say another word, I snapped his picture. I got him with his mouth wide open.

"If I was back home," I said, "I could print this picture out for you, but if you look at this screen, you'll see how it looks."

Ney and the other generals moved up to look over their leader's shoulder at the camera screen.

"Incredible!" Napoleon said. "This is a miracle!" He handed me back the camera. "It's a terrible portrait of you, captain. You look like an oaf.

"*I* will show you how it's done," he said, striking his famous pose.

I snapped his picture. He immediately grabbed the camera from me. "This is magnificent," he said. "I'll never have to sit still again." He struck another pose. "Once more!"

I was about to snap the second photo when a lieutenant burst into the tent. "Your Excellency," he shouted, "the British are advancing!"

"Not now!" Napoleon snapped. "This is for posterity."

"General," Ney said, stepping forward, "*the British are advancing!*"

"Well," Napoleon replied, "take your cavalry and go charge them. What do you think I gave you a cavalry for?"

Ney seemed taken aback. "General…?"

Napoleon turned to his military staff. "All of you, go! Charge! Fight! *Kill!*

"Monsieur Bullock and I have a secret plan we wish to discuss."

"We do!?!" I said.

"Go! Go! *Go!*" Napoleon said, waving everybody but Gaspar and me out of the tent, and then donning his hat. "Monsieur Bullock, you say you are from…?"

"Louisiana, sir."

"Did you know that I used to own it? Sold it to finance my European 'expansion.'"

"Expansion can be expensive, sir," I said. "When my folks added an extra bedroom…"

"I was cheated!" he shouted. "Your President Jefferson, he was a great man. Big penis, but it was crooked.

"He gave me a paltry four cents an acre for that land. *Four cents!*"

Outside, the sound of cannon fire was becoming more intense.

"I will take it back!"

"Take 'what' back, sir?" I asked.

"Your 'Louisiana Purchase.' I will buy it back."

"Sir, that's about one-third of the United States."

"So?"

"I don't think you could afford it at today's prices."

"What?" Napoleon looked astounded. "They'd want more than four cents an acre!?!"

"A bit."

"Perhaps we can reach a compromise. That's what diplomacy is all about, isn't it?"

I was confused. I wasn't quite sure what he was getting at. And, then he told me.

"You take me back to your 2011."

"What!?!" I said.

"It's the first part of my plan," he continued. "I want to meet with your President. I guess it would be Jefferson's great grandson by now."

I couldn't believe what I was hearing. Bringing Napoleon back to 2011 would be so much better than merely having a photograph.

Perhaps it was the explosion of the cannon ball just outside of the tent, but before I gave the idea any serious thought, I agreed. "You need to be within two feet of me," I explained, inputting the proper coordinates into my time transmitter.

"And where exactly will we be going?"

"Right where I left from," I said, "or thereabouts."

"Gaspar, my sword!" Napoleon said.

Gaspar grabbed the weapon and hurried over to his boss, just as I pressed the "Activate" button.

"Wait!" I said, suddenly realizing what I was doing. "I can't do this. I can't change history."

"Don't worry, my young friend," Napoleon said, as the three of us started to dematerialize into the yellow glow. "I can."

And then, clutching the history book to his chest, he started singing that goddamn Italian opera again.

He was still singing it when we rematerialized on the 50-yard-line inside the football stadium.

But, the stadium wasn't empty this time. Once again, *damn it*, I'd configured my settings wrong.

I'd left 2011 on a Thursday, but now it was Saturday afternoon, halftime at the football game. The stadium was full. A marching band and cheerleaders were entertaining the enthusiastic crowd.

Napoleon stopped singing. "I think Louisiana has changed," he said. "Such a reception! How did they know I was coming?" He marched forward, waving to the crowd.

Several students spotted him. They started laughing and waving back, thinking that he was another student, in costume and part of the halftime show.

"I don't like this," Gaspar said, as we hurried along behind Napoleon.

I saw Rebecca sitting in the stands. She was seated two rows behind Professor Steele-Shaw, Dean Whitaker and an Air Force General. They were all staring in our direction. Steele-Shaw looked like he wanted to strangle me. The others looked simply bewildered.

"I want to say something to the peasants," Napoleon said.

"That's not a good idea," I said.

"Nonsense! They are my subjects. They love me!" He turned to the crowd. "Citizens!" he shouted.

I took hold of his arm. "Sir," I said, "we have to get out of here… *now*!"

"Why?"

"Because, if we don't, they are going to put us all away."

"The young man is correct, General," Gaspar said.

Gaspar and I each took Napoleon by an arm and started hustling him off the field, heading toward a side exit.

"Unhand me!" he demanded.

"Sir," I tried to explain, "this is 2011. People think you're dead."

"But, they can see that…*I am alive!*"

As we reached the exit, I spotted Steele-Shaw leaving the stands and rushing after us. He caught up with us in the parking lot. We were about to get into my car, which had been sitting there since Thursday. "Bullock!" he shouted, grabbing my arm. "What's going on here? Who is this clown?"

[I don't think Napoleon took kindly to being called a "clown."]

What the hell! "This is Napoleon Bonaparte," I said with a shrug.

"And, you are…?" Napoleon said graciously, extending his hand.

Steele-Shaw slapped his hand away. "Don't give me that…" he said before Gaspar grabbed him by the throat.

"Do not touch the emperor!" the valet said, picking up Steele-Shaw with a minimum of effort and tossing him over a car. He landed on his butt.

"Oh, shit!" I thought, as I hustled Napoleon and Gaspar into my Toyota. "Am *I* in trouble…"

For the next two or three hours, both Napoleon and Gaspar reminded me of my five-year-old nephew the time I took him to Disney World. Their eyes were wide, their mouths open, as they gazed with wonder and awe at the marvels of the modern world.

Napoleon wanted to know why there were no horses pulling my Toyota, or any of the other cars on the road. I explained to him that motors, not horses, powered automobiles, and he began to calculate how much money his army would save if they used cars instead of horses.

"That would depend on the price of gasoline," I said.

"Gasoline?" he said.

Back in my apartment, they were amazed by all of the extraordinary "boxes" that I owned. There was one that cooked my food, and another that kept it cold. There was also a "box" that played music and exhibited funny little pictures that moved. He was particularly enamored with a World War II John Wayne movie and also *SpongeBob SquarePants*.

But, what fascinated Napoleon the most was my "magic chamber pot". He kept flushing and flushing my toilet over and over again, watching the water in the bowl swirl away and then refill.

"How convenient," he said. "A world run by boxes. I will take some of these boxes back with me."

"Please don't forget the magic chamber pot, sir," Gaspar said.

"*That* above all."

"Unfortunately, Napoleon, sir," I said, feeling that I had to inject a note of reality into this surrealistic situation, "these modern conveniences won't work back in your time."

"And, why is that?"

"The toilet…'magic chamber pot'…requires plumbing, running water, and everything else needs power."

"Power?"

"Electricity…nuclear energy…"

"Is that like those nuclear missiles?" Napoleon asked.

"Nuclear power can be used for many purposes."

"I see," Napoleon said, pondering for a moment. "Well, I'll just have to talk to your president about that."

"Sir," I said, "it's not that easy to talk to him…these days."

"Nonsense!" Napoleon said. "I am a Head-of-State. He is a Head-of…"

"But," I interrupted, "in 2011, you're dead!"

"Why do you keep saying that?"

"It's true, General," Gaspar said.

"Sir," I said, "if you go out and start telling people that you are Napoleon Bonaparte, they'll think you are crazy."

Napoleon smiled. "But, my dear boy," he said. "I *am* crazy. How do you think I conquered most of Europe?"

"They would put you away," I persisted. "Our insane asylums are full of people who think they are Napoleon."

"All imposters!" he shouted so loud that I almost jumped. "I am the *real* Napoleon Bonaparte, and I want to speak to the President!"

What the hell! "Fine," I said. "We'll call him." I picked up the phone and asked for Washington, D.C. Information. "The White House, please."

Napoleon looked at Gaspar. "Who is he talking to?" he said. Gaspar shrugged.

I got the White House operator on the line, and then handed the phone to Napoleon. "Speak in here," I explained. "Listen there."

Napoleon heard the operator's voice, and then asked:

"Is somebody inside this thing?"

"She's in Washington, D.C.," I said.

He looked momentarily bewildered, but then he yelled into the phone, "This is Napoleon Bonaparte. I want to speak to the President of the United States."

Standing next to him, I could hear the click on the other end of the line as the operator terminated the call. "That woman is very rude!" Napoleon said.

"Sir," I said, "before anybody will believe that you are Napoleon Bonaparte, they first have to know that my time transmitter works."

"He's right, General," Gaspar said.

"Gaspar," Napoleon snapped, "you are supposed to agree with me! Not him!" He took a breath and then turned to me. "Monsieur Bullock," he said, "I came to your 2011 to meet with your President. If he refuses to see me, I would consider that to be a grave insult, and I would be forced to sever all diplomatic relations with the United States."

"Really?" I said, not quite sure how I should react to his statement.

And then, I was saved by the bell. The doorbell.

"Maybe you should wait in the bedroom," I said to my two guests, as I walked toward the door.

"You are expecting a mademoiselle?" Napoleon asked.

"No, nobody," I said. "They just might be shocked to see you."

"But, why…?"

"You're dead, sir," Gaspar said.

"Stop saying that!" Napoleon snapped. He let out a sign of resignation, then: "We will wait in the bed chamber."

"Thank you," I said.

"Gaspar," he said, exiting to the bedroom, "if we had some of those talking devices, we could eat all of our carrier pigeons."

Rebecca, my redheaded, blue eyed graduate student, was at the front door. "Professor Bullock," she said, looking quite worried, "are you okay?"

"I'm fine." I shut the door behind her. "The time transmitter…it works, and, this time, I have absolute proof."

"That's wonderful, Professor." She really didn't look convinced. "What kind of proof? Pictures?"

"Even better," I said.

"Professor, you're not talking about that person you had out on the field with you? The one who was dressed up like Napoleon?"

"Yes, I…"

"I was sitting right behind Dean Whitaker and Professor Steele-Shaw." Tears started to well up in her eyes. "They are *so* angry. They're talking about firing you."

She leaned her head on my shoulder and started to weep.

What could I do? I put my arms around her and held her close. It felt rather nice.

"Rebecca," I said, "That man is the *real* Napoleon Bonaparte. I brought him back with me from 1815."

"How can that be?" she said, pushing away from me. "He's been dead for almost 200 years."

"Dead!" Napoleon said, emerging from the bedroom. "Do I look dead to you?"

Rebecca didn't answer. She just looked at him, and then fainted.

I know that Rebecca wanted to believe me; wanted to help me. But, frankly, if our positions had been reversed, I probably would have been just as dubious as she was.

"Madmoiselle," Napoleon said to her after she'd regained consciousness and was sitting on the sofa, "I will prove to you that I am Napoleon. Ask me anything about myself and I will answer it."

Rebecca thought for a moment, then: "What's the name of the ship that took you to St. Helena?"

"I don't know," Napoleon said with a shrug. "I haven't gone there yet."

"Rebecca," I said, trying to be gentle. "You have to ask him about something that took place *before* Waterloo."

"What difference would that make?" she said. "Steele-Shaw will just say he's a history buff that has read and memorized every biography about Napoleon."

"She has a point," I said.

"My God, Gaspar," Napoleon said. "Why must I go through all this nonsense? All I want is to see the President."

"Professor," she said, the tears starting to return, "They're meeting at Dean Whitaker's house this evening. You're going to be fired."

"I'll go there before that," I said. "This afternoon. I'll talk to them."

"And, I will go with you, young man," Napoleon said.

I wondered if that was a good idea.

Rebecca stood up. "I've got a suggestion," she said.

"Yes, my dear?" Napoleon replied.

"It wouldn't be definite proof," she said to Napoleon, "but why don't you let us take your coat over to the Chemistry Department? They could run some tests to determine how old it is."

"What would that prove?" he asked.

"Would a look-a-like be wearing a coat that's two hundred years old?"

"She's right!" I said.

"Excellent!" Napoleon said. He removed his coat. "Would you like the pants, too?"

"No," Rebecca said. "The coat will do just…"

"Because," Napoleon interrupted, "you should be aware that I am a great man and a great man has a…"

"*General!*" Gaspar and I shouted in unison.

Napoleon got the message. "Pardon," he said, handing the coat to Rebecca. "I forgot myself."

"How long will these tests take?" I asked.

"I don't know," Rebecca said. "A few hours, maybe. I'll meet you at Dean Whitaker's."

"Splendid!" Napoleon said. "But first, perhaps we might dine? It would be embarrassing if I met with the President and my stomach was making funny noises."

"Sir," I tried to explain, "we're going to see Dean Whitaker. He's just head of the university's Physics Department."

"He's an important man, is he not?" Napoleon said. "An important man would know the President."

What the hell!

While Rebecca took the coat over to the Chemistry Department, I took Napoleon and Gaspar out to get something to eat. I was pretty hungry myself, since I hadn't eaten anything since I'd time traveled.

The general was insisting on having crepes, so I took him to IHOP; the one located far enough from the campus so that I wouldn't run into any of my students. It was also the best I could afford on a junior associate professor's salary.

We sat in a corner booth and, of course, everybody was staring at us.

Why shouldn't they? Napoleon, his head buried in the history book, was wearing one of my sport jackets, three sizes to big for him, and Gaspar looked like a giant fugitive from a Renaissance Faire.

"What is this!?!" Napoleon demanded when the waitress set a plate of pancakes smothered in strawberries and whipped cream in front of him. "These are not crepes!"

"Yes, they are," I said. "Just fatter."

He, begrudgingly, took a bite.

"Good?" I asked.

He didn't answer, just grumbled something, took another mouthful and then another.

Dean Whitaker lived in a colonial-style home in an old conservative area of the city. At one time, it might have been the master's house on a plantation.

"Okay, General," I said, as we walked toward the driveway, "this is the big test. If we can convince Dean Whitaker that my time transmitter works, you're well on your way to meeting the President."

"I will charm him," Napoleon said.

"That's what I'm afraid of."

Dean Whitaker was definitely displeased when he opened the door and saw my two companions. "Mr. Bullock," he said, "I don't appreciate your bringing your practical jokes into my home."

Before I could respond, Napoleon stepped forward. "Dean Whitaker," he said, gushing charm, "I am Napoleon Bonaparte. It is such a great honor to meet you on what will soon be, again, my Louisiana Territory."

"I beg your pardon?" Dean Whitaker looked befuddled.

"Your brilliant young colleague here," Napoleon said, putting his hand on my shoulder, "has made it possible for me to come and reclaim what was stolen from me in a fraudulent land deal."

"Bullock," Dean Whitaker said, "this is in very poor taste."

I started to explain, but then:

"Hey, is that that Napoleon fella?"

The Air Force General who had been sitting with Dean Whitaker at the football stadium strolled into the entry hall from the living room. A ruggedly handsome man in his early-sixties, his uniform jacket was unbuttoned, a cocktail was in his hand and he had a mellow expression on his face.

"School business, Bart," the Dean said, annoyed with the interruption.

"Hell," the Air Force General said, approaching the door, "I think it would be a hoot to trade war stories with one of the greatest military minds that the world has ever known."

"Bart, please…" Whitaker said, then to me with a sigh: "This is General Broderick, my brother-in-law."

Broderick ignored him. "'Course, General," he said to Napoleon, "you sure fucked up at Waterloo, didn't you?"

"That has yet to be determined," Napoleon said, recognizing a possible ally.

"You must be the geek who invented that time machine," Bart said, turning to me.

Before I could respond, he put his arm around Napoleon's shoulder and started escorting him toward the living room. Gaspar was right behind them. "What're you drinking, General?" Broderick said.

"A glass of brandy would be nice."

"That's right," Broderick said. "You're one of them Froggies."

"Actually," Napoleon said, "France is my adopted country. I was born in Corsica."

"Corsica, huh?" Broderick pointed at me. "Stay put, son. You and I are gonna talk."

"Tell me, General," Napoleon said. "Do you know the President?"

"Hell, yes! He visited my missile base 'bout five months ago."

"Missile base?" Napoleon beamed as they disappeared into the living room. "You must tell me all about it."

Dean Whitaker turned to me. "You might as well come in," he said.

"Sir," I said, "if you'll just give me ten minutes, I'm sure I can convince you that really *is* Napoleon Bonapate."

"Mr. Bullock," he said, "even if I accepted your theory of time travel—which I don't—what you have sitting in my living room is not even science-fiction. It's fantasy."

"Your brother-in-law seems to be accepting it."

"Put a pair of ears on the man and my brother-in-law would accept him as Mickey Mouse. Haven't you figured out yet that he's an imbecile?"

"But, he's an Air Force General…."

"He's *still* an imbecile."

Inside the living room, Napoleon and General Broderick were sitting across from each other. We watched them, drinking and chatting away like a couple of old war buddies.

"You know, General," Broderick said, "if you had a couple of our ballistic missiles back at Waterloo, you could've whipped ol' Wellington's ass."

"That is my opinion, too."

"Serve the damn tea drinker right," Broderick said with a snicker.

Napoleon stood up. "General Broderick," he said, "you are a man with a large penis."

"Look, fella," Broderick said, a bit taken aback, "I know military policy has stopped the 'Don't Ask, Don't Tell,' but I want you to know that I don't go in for that kinda thing."

Napoleon seemed amused. "No, General, you misunderstand," he said. "I mean to say that you are a great man, and a great man must have a…"

"Oh!" Broderick said, getting his drift. "Yeah, well…I don't like to brag, but back when I was a captain, I'd be in the locker room and even my senior officers were tempted to salute."

As Broderick and Napoleon shared a laugh and refilled their glasses, Dean Whitaker stormed into the living room. "Napoleon or not, this man is absolutely insane," he said to his brother-in-law. "What does he expect us to do? Give him back the whole center third of the United States?"

"Well," Napoleon said, "yes."

"Alfred," Broderick said to Dean Whitaker, "this is a Government matter. Let me handle it."

Dean Whitaker rolled his eyes in exasperation and walked back to me in the entry hall.

"See, General," Broderick said to Napoleon, "it's not as simple as all that. Since you sold us that Louisiana Territory, it's appreciated in value."

"Appreciated?" Napoleon said.

"Yeah, it's like if you bought a Picasso…."

"Picasso?"

"Don't you know your Frenchy painters?"

Napoleon shook his head and shrugged.

"Anyway," Broderick continued, "before he was famous, Picasso probably sold his stuff for five bucks and a bottle of wine. But, then, over the years, them paintings appreciated in value. And now, they're worth, hell, millions. It's the same thing with real estate."

"I understand that," Napoleon said, "and I want to be fair. Certainly you're entitled to a profit. You paid me four cents an acre. I will give you eight."

Broderick chuckled. It was an uneasy chuckle, but a chuckle. "We got millions of people living there," he said. "What're we supposed to do with them?"

"General," Napoleon said, "we're both military men. When have 'people' ever stopped us from occupying real estate?"

"You're right!" Broderick said with a guffaw.

"See!" Dean Whitaker said to me. "He's not only insane. He's dangerous!"

"It wasn't supposed to go this way," I said.

"Hey, Geek," Broderick said. I could see the wheels spinning in his head as he walked toward me. "Tell me more about this time machine."

"Careful," Dean Whitaker cautioned. "Do you want to destroy your entire career for these two madmen?"

The bell saved me again. Actually, it was two bells. The doorbell and the telephone.

The *good* news was that Rebecca was standing at the front door. The *bad* news was that Steele-Shaw was standing right behind her.

"Raymond," Dean Whitaker said, "this is a mess."

"You're telling me?" Steele-Shaw said. "They're talking about Bullock, his time machine and this Napoleon look-alike all over campus."

"They are?" I said, somewhat surprised.

"Bullock," Steele-Shaw said. "You're through!"

"Wait!" Dean Whitaker said. "The important thing is that the press doesn't get this story."

Mrs. Whitaker, a full-figured lady who always seemed to be smiling, hurried in from the kitchen. "Alfred," she said, "a reporter from the *Evening Standard* is on the phone."

Dean Whitaker smiled daggers in my direction. "Get a number," he said. "I'll call him later."

"Yes, dear," Mrs. Whitaker said. She started back toward the kitchen, then: "Is Mr. Napoleon staying for dinner?"

Her husband answered with an emphatic *"No!"*

"Don't worry," Broderick whispered to Napoleon, who had joined him in the entry hall. "My sister's a lousy cook anyway."

"This whole thing is a hoax," Steele-Shaw said.

"That's not true!" I said.

"I spoke to Ms. Kaplan here," Steele-Shaw continued. "I know about the coat. It's been tested, and it's not more than a year or two old."

"What do you expect?" Napoleon said. "An emperor does not wear hand-me-downs."

Steele-Shaw pointed to Napoleon. "And, where did Bullock dig you up? In some amateur theatrical company?"

"Damn it!" I insisted. "My time transmitter *does* work and this *is* Napoleon Bonaparte!"

"Excuse me," Rebecca said. "There's something else about the coat."

"What is it, Miss Kaplan?" Dean Whitaker asked.

"The dye. It's a kind that hasn't been used in garments for over a hundred years. Not even in theatrical costumes."

I beamed at Rebecca. She returned the smile.

"That doesn't prove anything," Steele-Shaw said. He suddenly blanched when he saw Gaspar step out of the living room. "That man!" he said, pointing at the valet. "He assaulted me."

Napoleon grinned. "Yes, he did, didn't he?"

"I'm going to have you both arrested," Steele-Shaw said.

"Now, just a minute," Broderick said, stepping forward. "If we're talkin' time machine here, then we're talkin' about somethin' that should be under military control."

"There *is* no time machine!" Steele-Shaw shouted.

"Bart," Whitaker said to his brother-in-law, "please stay out of this."

"My time transmitter isn't a weapon, General," I said.

"Maybe not, son," he replied, "but in the wrong hands, it could be used as a weapon. I mean, what if some Nazi skinheads got hold of it? They could go back and give Hitler our D-Day invasion plans."

"Bart…" Dean Whitaker pleaded.

"Or," Broderick continued, "one of them damn radical Indian groups. You want them turning the tables on General Custer?"

I bit my lip, trying not to smile. I think that Dean Whitaker, Rebecca and Steele-Shaw must've done the same.

"I mean," Broderick said, his face flushed, "worse than they actually did."

"It could've been worse?" Rebecca said, and then started to giggle.

"Bart," Whitaker said, "it hasn't even been determined yet if the device is genuine or not."

"The military can determine that," Broderick said.

"Nevertheless," Dean Whitaker said, "whatever it proves to be, Bullock's invention *is* university property."

General Broderick ignored him and took hold of my arm. "Son, I'd like you and the General here to accompany me over to the missile base for a debriefing."

"I don't want to go to any military base," I said.

"Nonsense," Napoleon said. "We would be delighted to visit your base, General."

"Excellent!" Broderick said.

"And, will I get to see the missiles?"

Broderick finished off his drink and buttoned up his uniform jacket. "Sure, why not?" he said.

"And, the President might join us?"

"Whatever..." Broderick said.

So, even though I kept protesting, off Napoleon, Gaspar and I went in General Broderick's BMW, heading for a secret missile base over sixty miles away.

Professor Steele-Shaw did try to stop us, but before he could lay a hand on anybody, Gaspar grabbed him. "Do not touch the General," he said, and then he tossed him across Dean Whitaker's driveway.

"Nice move, soldier," Broderick said over his shoulder to the massive Gaspar, as we drove away from the house.

"He is my valet," Napoleon said from the back seat. He buttoned up his own coat that he had retrieved from Rebecca.

"Valet?" Broderick said. "How does he press your clothes? Sit on them?"

We were on the road for well over an hour, mostly driving through bayous and some farmland. For almost the entire journey, Napoleon kept singing that Italian opera in his off-key falsetto voice. My head was splitting, and I think that his performance was having the same effect on Broderick. At one point, the General leaned over and whispered, "Doesn't he know any Hank Williams?"

"Not even Andrew Lloyd Webber," I said.

We'd been traveling for about two miles down a badly paved, rural road. We passed a small, frame house, its paint peeling, and then turned into the gated driveway of a large fenced property and stopped. Trees and other foliage in front of the fence blocked any view of what was inside.

"Is this the base, General?" I asked.

"Yeah, but it's well camouflaged."

"Don't your neighbors object to having nuclear weapons so close to them?"

Broderick pressed a button on his dashboard and the gate swung open. "As far as they know," he said, "I'm just an eccentric, reclusive millionaire."

As we started through the gate, I glanced at the small house across the road. An elderly African-American couple stood on the front porch, holding an American flag and waving at us.

Inside of the fence, hidden from the road, was a handsome estate that looked like it was once a large plantation. A winding driveway, surrounded by rolling green grass, led up to the Colonial-style house, something right out of *Gone with the Wind*.

"You've certainly got a large gardening staff," I said, noting a half-dozen or so groundskeepers, each wearing a long backpack.

"And they're all armed with the latest assault weapons," Broderick said. "Bet you can't guess where we hide the missiles."

Napoleon, Gaspar and I all spoke in unison: "Under the lawn," we said.

Broderick seemed disappointed. "Well, yeah…"

He pulled up in front of the mansion and stopped. As we got out of the car, two men, obviously security guards, in civilian clothes, emerged from the house. Each had a sidearm.

"I'm not comfortable with this," I said, perusing my surroundings.

"It's certainly not as large as my palace," Napoleon said.

"Gentlemen," Broderick said, "please come in. My home is your home."

"I think I'd like to go back to the University," I said.

"Come on, boy," Broderick said. "We're just going to have a little talk."

I started to back away from him. "No," I said, "I'm going home now."

"Sergeant," Broderick said to one of the security guards, "Please escort Professor Bullock to our guest quarters."

"Yes, sir," the man said. He started toward me.

"Wait a minute!" I said, retreating at a slightly quicker pace. "I'm a United States citizen and you have no right…"

"You're a threat to our national security, boy," Broderick said.

"General," Napoleon said, stepping forward, "if I may…?"

"Go ahead," Broderick said. "Reason with the geek."

Napoleon approached me and gently took me by my arm.

"They're going to lock us up," I said to him.

"Tom…Tommy," he whispered, as we started to stroll along the lawn, away from the front porch. "Don't do this. I need you here if my plan is to work."

"What plan?" I said. "If you want to see the President, General Broderick can get you to him a lot quicker than I can. But, if you think they're going to give you back the whole central part of the United States, you *are* crazy."

"Not *that* crazy," he said. "I have no intention of foreclosing on the United States."

"Then, what?"

He shook his head. "Not yet," he said. "But I do need you."

"I don't know what for," I said, totally despondent. "I wish I'd never invented that damn time transmitter. Ever since I started developing it, it's caused me nothing but problems. My career is in the toilet…"

"Tommy," Napoleon said, "a man must believe in himself before he can achieve greatness. And you, my dear young man, are a great scientific genius."

"It's nice of you to say that, but…"

"Did you know," he interrupted, "that when I was a young lad, my father sent me to a military academy in France? I was the only Corsican in the school. The other boys ridiculed my manner…my speech. But, I knew inside that I was smarter than they were. I knew that, someday, I would be leading them into battle. And, I did."

"You never doubted yourself?"

"Of course not! I had the greatest penis in the school."

"But, of course," I said. I started to laugh.

"Now," he continued, "let's go in and placate this moronic general with the large penis. Notice that I did not say 'great'. And, I promise you, by the end of the day, you will be hailed as the greatest scientific mind since your Eli Whitney."

"Whitney!?!" I said, as we headed back toward Broderick and his men, who were eyeing us from the front porch. "The cotton gin!?!"

"He also invented muskets with interchangeable parts. More useful by far."

"Wow!" I said. "You learn something every day."

The inside of the mansion belied its exterior. What must once have been an elegant grand entry hall with a spiral staircase had been turned into the administrative headquarters for this Air Force missile base. There were two metal desks, one manned by an efficient-looking airman and the other by an efficient-looking airwoman, both dressed as domestic workers, and each was equipped with a sidearm. There were also two guards, dressed as butlers, on duty and they were carrying assault rifles.

"Outside may be a façade," Broderick said, as we entered. "But, in here, things operate like a military unit."

A uniformed major in his mid-thirties entered from a door beneath the stairs and approached us. "Sir," he said, "this is a restricted area. Have these people been cleared?"

"I'm clearing them, Major," Broderick said.

"But, who are they?"

Broderick smirked. "Don't you recognize Napoleon Bonaparte when you see him?"

The major stood open-mouthed, as we proceeded across the hall. The entire military staff, in fact, looked at us in astonishment.

"Tell me, son," Broderick said to me, "how does this time travel gizmo of yours work?"

"The transmitter emits an electromagnetic field that creates a wormhole that allows one to travel along the space/time fold."

"Fascinating," Broderick said. He didn't understand a word of what I said. "I'd like a demonstration."

"Oh, but first," Napoleon interrupted, "you promised to show me your missiles."

"So I did," Broderick said. "Major Collins!"

"Yes, sir!" the major said, hurrying over to us.

"Please escort Professor Bullock to the guest quarters while I give our honored guest here a guided tour."

"But…" I tried to protest.

"Relax, son," Broderick said. "The general and I got some 'grown-up' business here. No civilians allowed."

While Broderick, Napoleon and Gaspar stepped into an elevator— "another box" as Napoleon called it—Major Collins and the sergeant escorted me down a long hallway. He unlocked a door at the end of it, and I walked into a pleasantly decorated bed/sitting room with an old-fashioned canopy bed.

"Am I a prisoner?" I asked.

"The general said you were a guest, didn't he?" the major replied. "If you were a prisoner, the room wouldn't be this nice."

"I'm sure it wouldn't be," I said.

"Would you like something to eat?" the major asked. "Our cook makes a great gumbo."

"I hate gumbo," I said. "Gives me gas."

Our conversation was suddenly interrupted by the loud, grating sound of a siren, the truly frightening kind you hear in World War II movies when a Nazi Gestapo vehicle is coming to take you away.

"What is it?" I asked.

"Security breach!" Major Collins shouted over his shoulder, as he and the sergeant sprinted back down the hallway.

"Oh, Jesus!" I muttered to myself. I didn't really know what had happened, but whatever it was, I sure as hell knew who'd caused it to happen.

I also knew that I didn't want to be there. I followed Major Collins and the sergeant back down the hallway. I found them standing at the elevator door, anxiously waiting for it to open. Behind them, everybody else also looked quite nervous, and they all had their weapons out. Even the "groundskeepers" were rushing in from the outside, their automatic weapons ready to fire.

The elevator door opened and Broderick stormed out, boiling mad. His hat was askew, his uniform torn and disheveled. "Where is that little pissant geek son-of-a-bitch!?!" he shouted.

I ducked back into the hallway.

"General," Major Collins said, "what's happened?"

"That lunatic has seized the control room!"

"What lunatic?"

"Napoleon Bonaparte," Broderick said. "Who else?"

"How could he do that?" Collins asked.

"He ambushed us! Him and his valet. The big palooka tossed me and the control officers out of there like we were sacks of dirty laundry."

"My God!" Collins said.

"He's threatening to launch the missiles against Russia…Says it would serve 'em right."

Major Collins started for one of the desks. "I'll alert the Pentagon," he said.

Broderick grabbed his arm. "Don't alert the Pentagon," he said. "They don't have to know about this."

"Sir," Major Collins said, "if the missiles are launched, the Pentagon *will* know."

"Let's try to keep this situation contained as long as possible," Broderick said. "Careers are at stake here, Major. Mine *and* yours.

"With all due respect, sir, I didn't bring Napoleon Bonaparte into a highly secured area."

"I'll remember you said that, Major," Broderick said, turning away from him, and then spotting me standing in the hallway.

I didn't know what to say, so I just tried to smile. *Big mistake!*

"Sergeant," Broderick shouted, pointing directly at me, "shoot that man in the leg."

"What!?!" I said, retreating back down the hallway.

"I can't do that, sir," the sergeant said.

"Fine!" Broderick said, snatching an automatic rifle from one of the groundskeepers. "I'll do it!"

"You can't, sir!" Major Collins said, grabbing the rifle from him.

Broderick clenched his fists and screamed. "Is there no loyalty!?!" He glowered at the major. "You're lookin' at a court-martial , boy."

"Whatever, sir," the major said. "But, please, just calm down."

"I'm calm," Broderick said, anything but. "The geek there is responsible for this situation, and he's going to resolve it."

"He can't resolve it if you shoot him," the major said.

The major was a very smart man.

"Sir," the smart man continued, "even if 'Napoleon Bonaparte' has taken charge of the control room, the chances of his being able to launch a missile are pretty slim. He doesn't have the code."

"He broke open the code box," Broderick said.

"Still, he doesn't know how the system operates."

Broderick's face was beet red. "I gave him a demonstration," he mumbled.

"Oh, shit!" The major looked over in my direction. "Professor, would you please come here?" he said. "I promise nobody is going to shoot you."

"Until later," Broderick muttered.

The general, Major Collins and I adjourned to my "guest room," where I summarized for Collins the day's bizarre events. "That's really Napoleon Bonaparte down there?" he said. "And, he wants to rescind the Louisiana Purchase?"

Broderick lay on the canopy bed, staring up at the ceiling. "He said if we don't deed it back to him within two hours, he'll launch."

"That's ridiculous!" Collins said.

"And," Broderick said, "he wants the geek down there with him."

"I am *not* a geek," I said.

"You're responsible for him being here," Broderick said. He sat up on the bed. "This is treason!"

What the hell!

"I thought it was stupidity," I said, deciding to finally stand my ground. "He doesn't want the Louisiana Purchase. That's just a ploy."

"Then, what *does* he want?" Broderick said.

"He wants to defeat Wellington."

The sergeant suddenly bolted into the room. "Sir," he said, "the rocket engines… They've ignited!"

I think that everybody in the room blanched simultaneously.

We stepped off the elevator on the sub-basement of the facility to be greeted by Napoleon bellowing his Italian opera over the intercom. Outside of what was apparently the control room door, two slightly bruised security guards were holding their hands over their ears.

"What the hell is that?" Major Collins asked, as General Broderick, the sergeant and I hurried down the gray concrete hallway toward the metal door.

"He's singing," I said.

"The control room is impenetrable," Collins explained to me. "It's got its own oxygen and water supply, and there's enough food to last them a month."

"You talk them out of there, son," Broderick said, "and I'm sure we can get you a life sentence."

"Sir," Major Collins snapped, "you are not helping this situation." He turned to me. "Tell Napoleon that we're willing to negotiate his demands, but he has to shut down those engines *now*."

"Does he know how?" I asked.

"He turned 'em on," Broderick grumbled. "He should be able to turn 'em off."

"Tommy, my young friend!" Napoleon's voice blasted over the intercom. Obviously, he could see us via the security camera mounted above the control room door. "Come in! Everybody else go away, or I will push the big red button."

"Let 'im open the door, and then we'll rush 'im," Broderick said.

"And, what about the big red button, sir?" Collins said.

Broderick grumbled something I couldn't understand, and then everybody moved down the hall past the elevator, except me. The metal door slid open. I walked inside and it shut behind me.

If I didn't know I was in the missile control center, I'd have thought I was in a television studio. The bunker-like room had two large control boards filled with dials, buttons, switches and other gadgets. Each of the consoles was also equipped with a turnkey device and a big red button. There were also a half-dozen monitoring screens, giving a security camera's view of the sub-basement hallway, the outside of the mansion and the missile silo. One of the missiles looked like it was about to launch.

"Tommy," Napoleon said, "everything is going just as planned."

I looked at Gaspar. He was sitting in a swivel chair, shaking his head. "You have to shut down the rocket engines," I said to Napoleon.

"What rocket engines?"

I spotted a label on the control board, marked "Rockets." All of the switches were in the "on" position. "These rocket engines," I said, walking over to the board, switching them off and praying that I'd picked the correct switches. "You want to start a world war?"

"But, of course," Napoleon said. "Doesn't everybody?"

I looked at the television monitor. Thank God, the missile appeared to have gone dormant.

"General, sir," I said, "the people here are scared to death. What do you want?"

"I want to speak to the President and have him return my property to me."

"No," I said, "what do you *really* want? Modern weapons?"

Napoleon chuckled. "You are so smart, my young friend."

"Why didn't you ask them for that in the first place?"

"They would never have given them to me," he said. "This way, when I agree to forever relinquish my claim on the middle part of the United States, they'll think they are getting a bargain."

"General," I said, "I think you're in the wrong business."

Major Collins, General Broderick and the others hurried down the hallway as I emerged from the control room and the door slid shut behind me. "What does he want?" Collins asked.

"He'll settle for Kansas and Missouri," I said with a poker face.

"What!?!" Broderick and Collins said together.

"Just kidding."

Broderick shook his fist at me. "I'll Kansas and Missouri you if you do that again!"

"Come on, General," I said. "You deserved that."

"So, what does be want?" Collins said.

"He wants a wagon filled with automatic rifles, hand grenades and… what do you call them?… rocket launchers to take back home with him as souvenirs."

"How does he even know about these kinds of weapons?" Collins asked.

"He saw them on television."

"*On television!?!*"

"In a John Wayne movie."

"Damn it!" Broderick said. "I thought 'the Duke' was on our side."

"Oh, yes," I said, "and he also wants his own magic chamber pot."

Major Collins pondered a few moments, and then turned to Broderick. "What do you think, sir?"

"I think the little son-of-a-bitch *does* want to blast the damn tea drinker." Broderick said. "I say, give 'im the goddamn weapons. Let 'im blast that prissy Brit to Hell if he wants."

"General, you can't do that," I said. "If Napoleon defeats Wellington, it'll alter the course of history. This and us and everything else may not exist."

"Then," Broderick said, "let's just shoot the son-of-a-bitch."

"You can't do that either," I said. "Same reason."

"You're the scientist," Major Collins said. "You brought the man here. What do *you* suggest?"

"I suggest that you get him the weapons," I said.

"What?" Major Collins said. "But, you said…"

"I said, *'get'*. I didn't say *'give'*."

Major Collins wasn't sure he liked my idea. Neither was General Broderick, particularly since it meant that he was the one that was going to have to pull in a few favors from an old Army buddy in order to get the weapons. But, after I explained to them the rest of my plan, they agreed that that was probably to only course possible to resolve this situation.

There was no way that we were going to let Napoleon Bonaparte take a wagonload of modern weapons back to 1815. But, if we could make him believe he was getting the armaments, that would (*hopefully*) give us enough of a diversion, so that somebody could send him back to Waterloo before he knew what was happening.

Unfortunately, I was going to have to be that "somebody".

"This isn't right," General Broderick said. He gulped down another scotch. We were in his quarters off the entry hall, waiting for the Army to deliver the weapons.

"Sir?" Major Collins said.

"I don't care who that is down there. He's still a terrorist, and he's still holding the United States… no, *the world*, hostage."

"That may be so, sir," Major Collins said, "but if the professor's plan works, Napoleon and his companion will be gone in a few minutes and it'll be like this never happened."

Broderick poured himself another drink. "The son-of-a-bitch can still talk about it."

"What difference does it make if he talks about it back in 1815?" I asked. "Nobody would believe him. People would think he was delusional."

"It could still wind up in some history book," Broderick said. "What if my name came up in his delusions? What if he said he put one over on me?… We studied Napoleon at the Academy. If any of my classmates saw that book, I'd be laughed out on my ass."

I could see that Major Collins was struggling to keep a straight face. "Sir," he said, "if it's not in any history books now, then he didn't talk about it… Right, Professor?"

"Right!" I said, not really that sure.

The sergeant knocked on the door, and then entered. "The weapons are here, sir," he said.

General Broderick, Major Collins and I returned to the sub-basement of the facility. Just as we stepped off of the elevator, one of the security officers hurried over to us. "He's ignited the rocket engines again," he said.

"You're going to have to do this now," Major Collins said to me.

I punched the correct coordinates into the time transmitter. "I'll set it to activate in three minutes, okay?" I said.

"Whatever you say, Professor," Collins said. "You're the one who has to get out of there."

"This isn't gonna work," Broderick said.

"Sir," Collins said, "please let Professor Bullock do his thing."

"Listen," Broderick insisted. "You send that time transmitter thing back to 1815 or wherever, and what's to stop that lunatic from usin' it to come back here…or go any place else he wants?"

"He doesn't know the access code," I said.

"I still don't like it," Broderick mumbled. "It's humiliatin'."

"Sir," Collins said, escorting the general down the hallway, "let's get out of sight."

And, there I stood.

All by myself.

In front of the control room door.

The future of the world was in my hands.

I tried to pretend that I was Indiana Jones.

"You can do this," I told myself.

The control room door slid open and I walked inside. "Tommy," Napoleon said with a big grin, "I see that they have brought my new weapons." He pointed to a television monitor that gave an overhead view of an Army truck parked by the mansion's front porch.

"They're going to start unloading them in a few minutes," I said.

"Won't Wellington be surprised."

"General," I said, "you've fired up the rocket engines again."

"I know," he beamed. "The board is much prettier with the lights on."

"They're very upset out there."

"Tell them not to worry. If I get my weapons, I promise not to push the big red button."

My eye caught one of the monitors on the wall behind Napoleon and Gaspar. Thankfully, their backs were turned. Otherwise, they would have seen that General Broderick, pistol in hand, was edging his way down the sub-basement hallway toward the control room door. *The stupid jerk!*

I had to keep their attention on me.

"These code books here," I said, indicating two loose-leaf notebooks sitting on the control board. "They insist that I bring them out before they bring in the weapons."

"And, why is that?" Napoleon asked.

"They don't want them to go back with you," I said. "They're afraid that our future national security could be jeopardized."

Napoleon shrugged. "Take them," he said.

I gathered up the notebooks, and looked about for a spot to hide the time transmitter. There was none.

"You'll be back soon with the weapons?" Napoleon asked.

"Just a few minutes."

He walked over and embraced me. "Tommy," he said, "I am so delighted that you will be with me."

This was the perfect opportunity. I slipped the time transmitter into the pocket of Napoleon's large coat. Neither he nor Gaspar appeared aware that I had done it.

I glanced up at the monitor. Broderick was crouched right outside the door.

"The people of your time do not appreciate your genius as I do," Napoleon said.

"I know," I said, feeling a tinge of guilt.

I moved toward the exit. Napoleon, without looking at the monitor, pressed the button and the door slid open.

"Hold it right there!" Broderick said, bursting into the room, brandishing his pistol. He pushed me aside. "You're all under arrest for treason! *High* treason!"

Napoleon appeared to be amused.

"General," I said, "you can't do this."

"I'm in command here," Broderick said, "and I'm doing it."

We had to get out of there...*fast.* The clock was ticking on my time transmitter. It would be only seconds before everybody in the room would be transported back to 1815.

"No little twerp in a uniform is going to make me look like an idiot," Broderick said.

"General," Napoleon said with a smile, "how could I embellish what you already are?"

"You son-of-a-bitch!" Broderick bellowed. He pointed his pistol directly at Napoleon's head.

I couldn't let this mad general shoot Napoleon...even if Napoleon *was* crazy.

I tossed the notebooks at Broderick, hitting him in the face. His pistol fired, but the shot went wild.

"Do not hurt the General!" Gaspar said, grabbing Broderick's arm. They struggled with the pistol. Gaspar slugged Broderick, and the weapon went flying out of the control room. Another punch from the valet, and Broderick collapsed unconscious next to the control board.

Me?

I scooped up the notebooks and dashed outside of the room. As the door started to slide closed behind me, I heard Napoleon shout, "Gaspar! Your key! We launch!"

"No!" I yelled.

"Kick me out of Russia, will you!" Napoleon cackled before the door shut tight.

As Major Collins and the security officers rushed down the hallway toward me, we heard a rumbling sound. The concrete walls trembled, and we knew that a missile had been launched.

"Oh, Christ!" Collins said. "We've got to get in there."

The security officers trained their side arms on the control room door while Collins punched the security code into the keypad on the wall next to it.

The door slid open, just as the yellow glow inside began to fade away.

There was nobody in the room.

Collins rushed in and over to the control board. He pulled a series of switches, and then breathed a sigh of relief. "Thank God for the self-destruct option," he said.

"Where did they go?" one of the security men asked, looking around the empty control room.

"Hopefully, back where they came from," I said.

"And, the general...?"

All three airmen were looking at me for an answer, but all I could do was smile and shrug my shoulders.

You never read about all this in the newspapers or saw anything about it on television, because, frankly, the Air Force thought it would be too embarrassing for them if the story got out.

Who would believe it anyway?

I wasn't fired from the university. In fact, I was made a full professor...with tenure. That really bugged Professor Steele-Shaw, but when somebody is doing top-secret research for the Pentagon...

If you're wondering what happened to General Broderick...

The other day, Rebecca—she's my fiancée now—brought me a book, *The Last Days of Napoleon*. In it, there's a painting of a frail Napoleon on his deathbed. Several prominent-looking individuals surround him, but standing off to one side are two servants. One of them is definitely Gaspar, and the other is a rather imbecilic-looking fellow who looks remarkably like General Broderick.

Unfortunately, nobody in the painting is identified, so we'll never be sure.

I know what you want to ask me.

You want to know if I'm planning any more trips through time.

As I said, my work for the Pentagon is top-secret, but truthfully, I've been pondering Napoleon's theory about great men lately, and I can't help but wonder if it has any validity.

Were Julius Caesar and Alexander the Great really *great*?

I guess there's only one way I'll ever find out.

○

The Space Ship

After twenty days underwater, the space ship rose to the ocean surface and lay atop it like a huge whale basking in the sun.

Barnacles, seaweed and other remnants of the deep clung to the ship's once silver finish, now dulled by the saltwater.

"The horizon's clear, sir." The executive officer continued to peer through the hard, transparent shield that wrapped halfway around the top part of the vessel's pointed nose.

"The horizon is always clear on this damn planet," the captain replied from his command chair. "Test the atmosphere again."

"Yes, sir." The exec moved over to one of the crewmen at the ship's control console. "Begin testing sequence," he said.

The crewman flicked some switches on the console, turned a few dials, then reported, "Oxygen level is 20.8, nitrogen 77.4, sir."

"And how far are we from our point of departure?" the captain asked.

The exec studied one of the wall charts. "Just over two hundred leagues, Captain."

"Then we should be there on schedule," the captain said. "It will be good to get back home to Mother… I just hope she's there this time."

The exec approached the captain, lowered his voice. "A question, sir?"

"What is it?"

"The last few months, sir… You've seemed so angry. It's not like you. Is there something wrong?"

"Perhaps I'm just weary... frustrated," the captain said. For two years, we have been exploring this planet, and for what purpose?"

"To gather information, sir," the exec said. "Atmosphere, food sources, inhabitants.... Our future generations may be transported to one of these planets for settlement."

"We knew everything we needed to know about this planet eighteen months ago. We've circled these oceans... above the water, under the water... over a dozen times, and still Mother doesn't pick us up."

"She does have other planets to visit, sir. Other ships and crews to dispatch and recover."

"And, while she's doing that, we sail round-and-round-and-round this planet," the captain said. "Sometimes I feel like I'm back home in an amusement park, on a carousel.... When I was a child, I hated the carousel. I hated the wheel. I hated any ride that went nowhere and didn't take me to someplace new."

"With all due respect, sir," the exec said, "we weren't scheduled for retrieval until now. They didn't expect us to finish our work so early."

The captain perused the horizon. "This spot looks familiar," he said.

"Sir?"

"Isn't this the place where those funny little creatures attacked us? The ones in that strange vessel?"

"I think you're right, sir," the exec said, checking the charts. "It was about this time last year."

"One of them tried to climb up on the ship," the captain said, smiling for the first time in a month. "He even tried to puncture our hull with that spear or whatever it was he was carrying."

"We submerged before he could do any damage."

"That 'spear' could never damage this ship," the captain said. "And, if those creatures are this planet's chief inhabitants, then we will have no problem conquering it."

"I hope you didn't speak too soon, sir," the exec said. He pointed to a dark spec on the horizon.

The captain peered through the shield and squinted. "What is that?" he said, grabbing his binoculars.

"It looks like..."

"Well, I'll be damned," the captain said. He adjusted the focus on the glasses. "It looks like one of those strange vessels." He handed the binoculars to the exec.

"No, sir," the exec said. "It looks like the *same* vessel…and it's heading this way."

"Oh, my," the captain said, his smile turning malicious. "This could be invigorating."

"Sir," the exec said, "wouldn't it be more prudent if we just submerged right now?"

"Absolutely not," the captain said. "This has been the most boring voyage of my career. Before we leave this miserable planet, I want to have some fun."

"But, sir," the exec objected, "the safety of the ship…the crew…"

"The ship is perfectly safe from these primitive creatures," the captain said. "Just follow my orders."

"Which are…?"

"Nothing," the captain said. "Do absolutely nothing. After all, they're coming to us."

As the strange vessel sailed closer to the ship, the captain and the executive officer could see that it was, indeed, the craft that they had encountered a year earlier. It was made from what appeared to be wood and was apparently powered by wind, blowing into huge sheets of cloth strung out over tall poles that protruded from the vessel's center. About two dozen of the primitive creatures stood atop the deck of the craft, looking in the direction of the space ship. Their countenances were pale; their attire dark and cumbersome.

The vessel stopped about one hundred yards to starboard of the ship. The primitive creatures continued to stare in their direction.

"Look at that one," the captain said. He pointed to one of the creatures that was jumping around on the vessel's deck, flailing his upper limbs about.

The exec looked through the binoculars. "He appears to be angry."

"*Very* angry," the captain said.

"Isn't he the one that…?"

"That's right," the captain said. "He's the crazy one that tried to stab us with his spear."

"But, why would he come back?"

"Revenge."

As had happened a year earlier, three much smaller vessels were lowered from the deck of the larger one. Each craft was filled with eight to ten of the primitive creatures. They moved slowly, steadily through the water toward the space ship.

"See!" the captain said with a guffaw. "The 'crazy one' is in the lead vessel...and he's got his spear again."

"That's a bigger spear than last time," the exec said.

"So it is," the captain said.

"Sir," the exec said, "they're attacking. Don't you think we should take precautions...some action?"

"We will."

"When, sir?"

"When the prey have entered the trap."

"Sir?"

"Let the 'crazy one' climb aboard," the captain said. "Let him think he has won. And then, we'll submerge. Drown the son-of-a-bitch."

"Yes, sir," the exec said somewhat reluctantly.

"Have the crew stand by."

The first small vessel reached the nose of the space ship and, while the others remained behind, the "crazy one," brandishing his spear, clambered aboard. There was an odd protrusion extending from one of his lower limbs, which caused him to move with some difficulty up the nose toward the shield.

He reached the ship's wrapped-around window and glowered inside.

His wide, hate-filled eyes met the captain's, and the captain suddenly felt uneasy.

"Dive!" the captain shouted. "Dive, now!"

The "crazy one" grasped his spear with both hands, raised it above his head and brought it down with all his might onto the window.

The shield cracked.

He raised the spear again and smashed it down onto the window shattering it even further.

"Get us out of here," the captain shouted.

The ship began to submerge, moving forward. It struck the small vessel that had transported the "crazy one," capsizing it and spewing its primitive creatures into the ocean.

The jolt caused the "crazy one" to slip. He fell onto his back, but he did not let go of the spear. He raised it up once more and rammed it down into the shield.

This time, the lance penetrated, its tip just missing the captain.

The "crazy one" continued to grasp his spear as the ship proceeded to submerge. He was swept under the ocean's surface.

"We're taking on water," the exec shouted, as the ocean flowed in from the break in the shield.

"Surface!" the captain ordered, his uniform drenched. "We'll make repairs."

The space ship rose back up in the water. The ocean stopped pouring into the vessel, but the spear, the body of the "crazy one" still clinging to it, continued to protrude through the window shield of the craft.

The creature's wide, dead eyes stared at the captain.

"Ram them!" the captain said, pointing at the two other small vessels and the larger one that were all off the starboard. "Kill them all!"

"We can't engage them now, sir," the exec said. "We have to make repairs."

"I said, 'Ram them,' mister," the captain shouted. "Those creatures have done damage to my ship."

"Sir..." the exec continued to protest.

"Full speed!" the captain ordered.

The space ship plowed through the water. It destroyed the first small vessel, and then the second, smashing them both into pieces and propelling the primitive creatures aboard into the water and under its hull.

The captain cackled with delight, as he watched the helpless creatures disappear beneath the ocean's surface. "Now, the big vessel," he said. "Right through its center."

"Captain," the exec shouted. "You can't do this! Our shield is damaged. It won't withstand the impact!"

The captain said nothing, just looked in his direction for a brief moment. His eyes were wide and hate-filled, like those of the "crazy one."

He turned back forward to watch as the space ship crashed into the large strange vessel.

The impact forced the space ship's window shield to collapse inward from its frame. Its dagger-like shards stabbed into the captain, the exec and several of the crewmembers.

The space ship continued on through the vessel until the strange craft had been split in two, and all that remained were remnants of it floating on the choppy, swirling water.

Ishmael clung to the wood coffin that his friend, Queequeg, had had built for himself, and watched the giant beast sink below the ocean's surface.

Was that really a whale?

It did not look or behave like any whale he had ever seen before. Not even the legendary great white whale could act in such a manner.

But, what else *could* it be?

If he claimed that something other than a whale had sunk the ship, people would declare him to be mad and lock him up in an asylum.

Ahab, Starbuck, Stubb and the rest of the crew were dead.

He was the sole survivor of the *Pequod*, the only person who could relate its uncanny tale.

He prayed that he would be rescued soon, but not before he knew what that tale would be.

○

Bugsy's Boys

"I'm the guy who pulled the trigger on 'Bugsy' Siegel."

Maybe I should have kept my yap shut about that.

If I had, I wouldn't be where I am now at sixty-six: dyin'.

I'd probably still be dyin'. The two and a half packs I smoked every day and my bum ticker would have taken care of that, but I wouldn't be stuck out in the boonies in the Feds' Witness Protection Program.

They call me "Eddie C".

I was an "associate" of Jack Dragna. Back in the day, Jack ran the rackets in Los Angeles. They called him "the Al Capone of California".

I'd clipped a few guys for Jack. Small fry. They did a Houdini and nobody ever missed them.

"Bugsy" was different. Dragna hated the crazy Jew bastard ever since he'd tried to snatch control of the racing wire from him, but the guy was close with Lansky and Luciano, and that meant that he got a pass… until the Flamingo deal in Vegas turned sour. New York issued the order and Jack was delighted to get the contract.

He told me to "break the egg," and that's what happened on June 20, 1947. "Bugsy" was sitting in his living room, and I don't think he knew what hit him. Until I flipped, the Beverly Hills cops didn't know what had really happened either.

The hit made all the papers. Front page. Banner headlines. "Bugsy" was, after all, a celebrity, a Man of Honor. He was friends with big movie stars, like George Raft.

Me?

I laid low. I'd always liked playin' with numbers, so Jack stuck me behind a desk, had me do some bookkeepin' for his operations. He even had me paint his house once, and then he got pissed off because he didn't like the color.

The Feds were always tryin' to get Jack with their crime commissions and deportation orders. One time, they arrested him for screwing his "comare," his girl friend. Called it "lewd behavior".

But, Jack beat 'em. He dropped dead of a heart attack in 1956 before any of them government shysters could touch 'im.

Jack and me, we had our differences. But, he was okay. After he passed, I sort of faded away. I'd done pretty good in the stock market, so I retired. By the 1970s, I was 53 and livin'…with my 81-year old mother…in Agoura Hills, one of them new L.A. suburbs they were buildin' off the 101 in the late 1960s.

That's when I opened my yap when I shouldn't've.

The people in the neighborhood knew that I'd been "connected," but they thought I was just a bookkeeper, and I let 'em think that. Why should I make them afraid of me?

They called me "The Cat Man" because, aside from the three of my own, every night around five, I'd go up to this one corner with a bag of food and feed every stray cat in the neighborhood, dozens of 'em.

I just get mad when I see what people do to little animals. They just toss 'em out anyplace, on the road, in an empty field, in an alley, and leave them to die without thinking about the pain and suffering they're causing.

My mother, God rest her soul, she loved her flowers, but she hated the cats. "The fiori aren't going to put us into the poor house," she'd say. "But, my son, the stupido gatto man, will."

There was this kid in the neighborhood, David Goodman. He was in his late twenties, married to a looker and they had a young son. I figured him to be a mamaluke, or as "Bugsy" would've called him, a bit of a schmuck. But, he'd written a book about Clark Gable. I read a story about him in the local paper, and I got to thinkin'.

During the past few years, there'd been *The Godfather*, *The Brotherhood* and all them other books and movies about "the Mob". Most of 'em were bullshit, but somebody was makin' money off this stuff…and it wasn't me.

I was never a Made Man. There was no Omerta. After Jack had died, I'd been pretty much tossed aside, forgotten about, and most of the wiseguys I'd run with were, one way or the other, pretty much gone.

So, why couldn't *I* make up some fairy stories about "the Mafia"? If none of them were true, who was going to get hurt?

My problem was that I never finished high school and could hardly write a sentence. Mamaluke or not, I needed a *real* writer to help me.

I went to the bookstore and got my hands on a copy of Goldman's Clark Gable book, read it and then, one afternoon, I walked over to his house. He lived across the street from the elementary school.

He opened the door, dressed in jeans and a t-shirt. I could tell he was surprised and a bit uncomfortable to see me. "Eddie!" he says.

"I'm not interrupting anything am I?" I held up the copy of his book and a pen.

"What do you need? An autograph?"

"If you don't mind."

"Glad to," he says, leaning the book against the door and signing. "Thanks for buying the book."

"My pleasure," I say. I didn't have the heart to tell him I'd swiped it.

"Have a good evening," he says, handing me back the book and starting to close the door.

"I wanted to talk to you 'bout somethin', too," I say.

"Yeah? What's that?"

"Can we go inside? It's kinda private."

He hesitated a moment, then opened the door for me. "Sure," he says. "Come on in."

The kid's house was like a movie palace. There was these great old posters hanging on the walls, *Little Caesar*, *Key Largo*, *White Heat* and, on a table sitting against the wall, he had this statue that looked like The Maltese Falcon.

"Is that the *real* one?" I asked.

"Just a plaster copy," the kid says. "The real one would cost a fortune."

"I guess it would," I say. "I mean, with all them jewels…"

He offered me a beer, and then we went out onto his patio to sit by the pool. "So, what's up?" he says.

"You're a writer…"

"I know that."

"I wanna write a book, and I want you to write it with me."

"Everybody's got a book," he says, smiling.

"What?"

"I'm flattered, Eddie," he says. "What's it about?"

"You know, I used to be 'connected'."

"I'd heard that," he says, squirming a bit in his chair. "You were a bookkeeper or something."

"Or, 'something'," I say. "I want to write about them days."

"Won't that upset some people?" He kept squirming.

"The people I'm gonna talk about are long gone, and those that ain't… We can use phony names."

He sat there for a minute or two, scratching his beard. "I do love gangster movies," he says. "I just don't think that another book on the Mafia would sell right now."

"Why not?"

"It just seems that, since *The Godfather* came out two years ago, there's been twenty million books or movies on the subject. I think we're Mafia'd out."

I was afraid he was going to say something like that, so I played my ace. "What if my book tells something sensational?"

"Like what?" He took a swallow of beer.

"Like I'm the guy who pulled the trigger on 'Bugsy' Siegel."

The poor mamaluke, he turned white and I thought he was going to choke to death on that beer. "Are you serious?" he says, standing up and moving a step or two away from me.

I gave him a nod.

"And, you're willing to say that in print?"

"Why not?"

He moved further away from me. "Off the top of my head… When did it happen? Over twenty…."

"Twenty-seven years ago," I say.

"Right!" he says. "Well… There's no statute of limitations on murder, is there?"

"Statue of *what*?"

"*Statute* of limitations," he says. "They could still prosecute you. You *could* get the gas chamber."

I couldn't believe what this mamaluke was saying. "For whacking 'Bugsy'!?!" I say. "Hey, were not talkin' about Albert Schweitzer here. I figure I did the world a favor."

"That may very well be," he says. "I'm sure it is, but I doubt if the D.A. will look at it that way."

Mamaluke or not, this kid was no dummy. "Them prosecutors can be pretty narrow minded," I say. "Let me think on it for a day."

"Do that." He walked me down to his side gate that led out onto the street.

"You ain't gonna say nuthin' about this, are you?" I say.

He raised his hand, like he was taking the Omerta. "I swear," he says. He looked like he was about to faint.

"Good," I say, and then I left.

The mamaluke might have kept his yap shut, but what I didn't know is that he had a nosey neighbor, Nate Swanson. That son-of-a-bitch had been sitting in his back yard, on the other side of the wall, and he'd heard our whole conversation.

So, what does he do?

He calls the Beverly Hills cops.

I didn't know that for a couple of days.

I spotted Goldman and his five-year-old son tossin' a football around at the elementary school, so me and my three cats strolled over there to have a talk. "The kid's gonna play for the Rams," I say after the mamaluke had tossed him the ball.

He looked at me, a bit wary. "Hi, Eddie."

"Let's take a walk," I say.

Again, he turns white. "What's that?" he says. "A 'ride' without wheels?"

I couldn't help laughin' at that one. "I just wanna talk."

He tossed the ball back to his boy. "We can talk here," he says. "Nobody's listening."

I looked around, and nobody *was* listening. "If we did this book, why couldn't I use a phony moniker? A sudi-something…"

"A pseudonym?"

"Yeah, that," I say. "Nobody would have to know who I was, would they?"

"I'm not sure I want to get involved with this," he says. "My wife's uncomfortable…"

"You told *your wife*!?!" I couldn't believe it. I grabbed his shirt-front; cocked my fist.

"I tell my wife everything," he stammered.

I let him go, forced myself to relax. "It's okay," I say. "Mary's a right dame…. You tell her *everything*?"

"That's what marriage is about," he says, moving a step back from me. "Sharing."

"That's why I never got married."

"Mary's afraid of the repercussions a book like this might have," he says. "She doesn't want any 'Blackies' or 'Louies' showing up on our doorstep."

"Those guys won't bother you," I say. "They're all dead. Hell, I whacked a couple of them myself."

"*Don't tell me that!*" he says. He hurried over to his boy, who was kicking the football along the ground. "Patrick! Time to go!"

I called after him, "Think about it!"

I hung around the school grounds for a few minutes, pettin' my cats and watching some of the kids play, and then I headed home. As I came out onto the sidewalk, I saw a car parked in front of the ma-maluke's house and he was standing next to it, talkin' to this six-foot guy in slacks and a sports jacket, a copper if I ever saw one.

I can spot a copper a mile away. You show me twelve naked guys in a shower room, and I'll point out the copper every time. And, it's not just because they'll have the smallest dick. It's instinct.

The mamaluke spotted me watchin' him. He stopped talkin' to the bull and made a fast retreat for his house. I waited until "John Law" drove off, and then me and my cats strolled over to the mamaluke's front door and gave it a knock. "You been talkin' to the coppers?" I say when he opened the door.

He looked like he was going to pee his pants. "No," he says. "My next door neighbor has."

"Okay, I'll go talk to him," I say, turning to go.

Then, the mamaluke surprised me. "No!" he shouted, grabbing my arm and pulling me inside of his house. Maybe this kid was grow-ing some balls.

"You are not going to 'talk' to anybody," he says. "We don't do that kind of thing in this neighborhood."

"But, he's a canary," I say.

"He just overheard us talking the other day. He doesn't know who you are. I told the detective that I was acting out a scene from my novel."

"*What* novel?" I asked.

"I don't have a novel," he says. "I was bullshitting the copper to get rid of him." He started to laugh, but it wasn't the kind of laugh when you think something is funny. "'Copper'," he says. "Now, I'm talking like you."

"What's that flatfoot gonna do in six months or so, when you don't come out with no book?"

"I don't get your point?" he says.

"He's gonna know you were bullshitting him," I say, "and he'll be back to grill you again. 'Cept, next time, he won't be so polite."

The mamaluke didn't have no answer for that one.

Five minutes later, we were sittin' in his kitchen and he was, a bit reluctantly, on the phone to his New York book agent. "We're gonna get rich on this deal," I told 'im.

"Dead, too," he says.

He told the agent that he wanted to write a book called *The Man Who Shot "Bugsy" Siegel*. I liked that title.

I mean, I'd seen that John Wayne movie, *The Man Who Shot Liberty Valance*, and that was sure a winner. I got to thinkin', in a movie, maybe John Wayne could play me.

The agent, his name was Artie Baker, told the mamaluke that he'd start callin' the book editors first thing in the mornin', so David says he'd get in touch with me as soon as he heard something. After that, I left… thinking about what kind of new Caddy I should buy with my advance check.

They say that what you don't know can't hurt you, but that's a load of crap.

What I didn't know this time was that this Artie Baker fella was a bum. The last book he'd tried to sell was called *Queen Victoria and Jack the Ripper: A Love Story*.

Not even the *National Enquirer* would buy that one.

Anyway, he got on the phone the next day with this book editor and pitched the mamaluke's book…*my* book.

You know what he called it?

From "Bugsy" Siegel to The Kennedys to Martin Luther King: The Killer Talks.

What the bum didn't know is that that particular publisher was a Mob front. It was one of their legitimate businesses.

So, the editor stalls the bum, tells him to send her a written proposal (*whatever that is*), then the minute she gets off the phone, she calls her bosses…and they call *their* bosses…

But, what *they* don't know is that the Feds knew all about their operation, and they had their phone lines tapped.

You see where this is goin'?

A couple of days go by. I'm at my usual corner, feedin' my army of cats, when the mamaluke comes up to me. "I just talked to my agent," he says. "He's got a publisher interested."

"Sensational!" I say, but I could tell that there was somethin' bothering him.

"What do you know about the Kennedys?" he asked.

"Great men," I say. "Voted for both of 'em.…JFK six times." I gave him a wink.

He didn't smile. "And Martin Luther King?"

"Liked him, too, but I don't think I ever voted for him. Did he run for something?"

"I'm talking about their assassinations," he says.

Now, *that* pissed me off. "Hey," I say, "I had nothing to do with those. I'm totally clean."

"Relax," he says. "I didn't think you did."

That was a relief. Next, I figured he was gonna say I shot Lincoln. "Then, why'd you ask?" I say.

"My agent mentioned them."

"Maybe we'd better *talk* to your agent."

"*No*, Eddie!" he says, pointing his finger at me. This kid was *really* growing some balls. "Besides, he lives in New York."

"Kid," I say, "I swear 'Bugsy' was my last job. I quit right after that one."

"Why?"

"It was too big a hit. I had to lay low, otherwise I'd've had Bugsy's boys chasing me for the rest of my life."

"They *would* want to avenge their boss," he says.

"Naw, that wasn't it," I say. "I'm talkin' about the crazies *like* Bugsy.… If 'Bugsy' Siegel didn't like you, he'd smile…say 'hello'… slap you on the back…stick an ice pick through your eye…then pour you a martini."

"A real Mr. Charm," the kid says.

"There were plenty of nutcases out there just like him," I say. "Still are. 'Bugsy's Boys'. If one of 'em whacked me, the guy who got 'Bugsy', he'd make a great rep for himself."

"Are they *still* after you?"

"No way," I say. "When I retired, the Bosses put out the word. Eddie C is a civilian, now. Leave 'im alone."

Out of the corner of my eye, I spotted a black sedan, the kind with the dark tinted windows, moving up the street in our direction.

"Of course," I say to the kid, "all that could change."

The sedan was moving slow. I do not like black sedans with dark tinted windows, particularly the slow ones.

"Get outta here!" I say to the kid.

"What?"

"Scram!" I say. "You're making the cats nervous."

"What are you talking about?" he says. One of the cats was rubbing against his leg. "Animals like me."

"So does your mother," I say. The sedan was getting closer. I gave the kid a push. "Move!"

"Screw you!" he says, and walked away in a huff.

"Wouldn't want your wife to get jealous," I shouted after him.

At that point, he spotted the sedan, and got my message. "Okay, Eddie," he says. "Whatever you say... Friends of yours?" He didn't wait for an answer, just headed back toward his house, quickening his step, as he got further away.

The sedan stops next to me, and out of the passenger side steps Sam "The Nose" Kaplan, a guy who, back in the day, was also a soldier for Dragna. Sam was a one-time boxer who seldom won a fight. He had a nose like Jimmy Durante's, which is how he got his nickname. These days, Sam wore a suit and, as I'd heard, he was skipper of his own crew.

"Hello, Eddie," he says, flashing a smile and making me wonder why he'd never gotten that broken tooth fixed.

"Long time," I say. I shook his hand. "What brings you here, Sammy?"

"I was on my way home," he says. "Thought I'd stop by, say 'hello'."

"Don't you live in Vegas?"

"I do."

"That's in the other direction," I say. "*Way* in the other direction."

Sammy turned to his muscle, a swarthy six-footer wearing sunglasses who'd just stepped out of the driver's side of the car. "Damn it, Dante," he says, "I told you you took the wrong turn."

Dante just stood there; didn't even twitch.

"He gets lost sittin' on the crapper," Sammy says to me.

"Good help is hard to find," I say.

"So, Eddie," Sammy says, "I see you're still with the cats…. Still makin' dough on the stock market?"

Sammy was never good at makin' small talk, so I decided to cut to the chase. "Whatcha doin' out here, Sam?" I say.

"Can't I visit an old friend?"

"No," I say. "Whatcha doin' out here?"

"Somebody's talkin' outta school, Eddie," Sam says. "About things they ain't supposed to talk about."

"You don't say."

"I hear tell they're writin' a book."

"Really?" I say, totally deadpan.

"What do you know about it?" Dante says. His voice sounded like he'd swallowed gravel.

"Dante," Sammy snapped, not even looking in his direction. "Who's in charge here?"

"You are, Boss."

"Then keep it shut!"

"Yes, Boss." Dante just stood there; didn't even twitch.

"Sorry about that," Sammy says to me.

"He's young." I say.

"You don't know anything about this book thing, do you, Eddie?"

"I'm no rat," I say, still deadpan.

"Didn't think so, but you're one of the few guys left from the old days, and I had to ask."

"I don't even *like* rats."

"My best to your mother," Sammy says, heading back to the car. "And the cats."

Watching them drive off, I did feel a tinge of guilt, but then I remembered that I really didn't owe these guys nuthin', and that was the end of the tinge.

I walked over to the kid's house and knocked on the door. No answer, and the lights inside were off.

I knocked again, harder this time. Still no answer, but I thought I heard the mamaluke inside going, *"Shhhh!"*

Did my temper boil at that one. I was tempted to just kick the goddamn door in, but I didn't want to get collared for breakin' and enterin', and besides, the mamaluke had a kid and I didn't want to scare him. I figured I'd pay 'im a visit at his office, and we'd have our own little sit-down.

Next day, I drove into town. The mamaluke had an office on the Sunset Strip on the third floor of one of them buildings where the glass elevators are on the outside.

He may have written a book, but his *real* job was bein' a press agent, getting the names of famous people in the papers, so that they'd be even more famous. I guess he was pretty good at it, because he had his own business.

Maybe he wasn't *that* good, 'cause he worked by himself. Didn't even have a secretary.

He was at his desk, on the phone, when I strolled into his office and, like before, he turned white when he saw me. "Hi, Eddie," he says. "What're you doing here?"

"You been ducking me, kid?"

"Whatever gave you *that* idea?"

"Your phone's always busy," I say, sittin' across from him, "an' when I come and knock on the door, the lights go out inside and nobody answers."

"I *was* a little nervous about those guys who came to see you."

"They're old friends," I say. "They stopped by to shoot the breeze."

"And, I just heard that my agent got mugged. They beat him up pretty bad *in his own office.*"

"Offices are dangerous places," I say. "Besides, he had a big mouth."

"This is getting a little *too* hairy," the mamaluke says. "I'd like to pass on the book."

"What're you talkin' about?" I say. "You're a writer. This is research."

"I'm not that kind of writer," he says. "*Hemingway!* He was that kind of writer. He went to Spain, Africa, fought in wars, ran with the bulls... Can you see *me* running with the bulls?"

"Hell," I say, "I ran from the bulls plenty of times."

"*With!*" he shouted, jumping to his feet. "Not *from!*"

"I wouldn't let nuthin' bad happen to you, kid," I say. "I like you."

"I know, but…"

"Hey," I say, deciding to change the subject, "you work with movie stars here, huh?"

He nodded, and then sat back down. "And, directors, composers… They pay me to get their names in the paper."

"I used to know a movie star," I say. "George Raft."

"Weren't he and Siegel best buddies?

"Yeah," I say. "Funny, I never hear from Georgie no more."

"Eddie," the kid says, "if you don't mind my asking, how did you get into this kind of work?"

"You mean, whackin' people?"

"Yeah."

"The Army taught me," I say. "I was in the South Pacific."

"But, that was war…"

"Hey," I say, "Uncle Sam gave me a trade. Somethin' I could use in civilian life."

"I know what you mean," he says, starting to laugh. "I had to take ROTC in college. You sat in class and they'd show you charts on how to kill a man with an axe."

"That's right," I say. "They teach you stuff you can use every day."

We both laughed at that one.

"Anyway," I say, "back home, I had an Uncle Joe in Chicago. He was 'connected'. He introduced me to the right people."

"Like Jack Dragna?"

"Right," I say, "but I never whacked nobody who didn't deserve it, or wouldn't've whacked me first if he had the chance."

"Bugsy deserved it?"

"He was skimmin' dough from his partners," I say. "A rat like that don't deserve to live."

"I guess," he says, turning to look out the window.

I could see that that conversation was over. I figured I'd give the kid a few minutes to stew. "Hey," I say, standing up, "where's your head?"

"Down the hall and around the corner."

"Be right back," I say and headed for the door. "Don't go nowhere."

I didn't witness what happened next.

Sure, I witnessed what I did in the can, but the kid told me what took place in his office right after I walked down the hall.

The kid was sitting at his desk, readin' the *Daily Variety*, when Sammy and Dante, the goon, walk in. Before the kid can even open his mouth, Dante grabs the front of his shirt and lifts him right out of his chair.

"Wanna talk to ya," Dante says.

Sammy tells the muscle to put the kid down, so Dante shrugs, then drops him back down so hard that the chair falls over backwards with the kid in it.

"Idiot!" Sammy says to the muscle. "I said no rough stuff."

"I thought he should know we mean business," Dante says.

The kid was probably ready to crap his pants when Sammy helped him to his feet and set him back down in his chair. "Sorry about that," he says. "We just wanted to ask you a couple of questions."

"Why didn't you just ask?" the kid says.

"I hear you're writing a book," Sammy says. "'Bout Benny Siegel… the Kennedys…that Luther King fella…"

"I never said *anything* about the Kennedys or Martin Luther King," the kid says. "That was my agent talking."

"Whatever," Sammy says. "What I want to know is…who's squealin'?"

"What?"

"Who's the canary? Where are you getting your dope?"

Now, here's where the kid proved himself to be a stand-up guy. These two goodfellas are standin' over 'im. He's on the verge of havin' a damn heart attack, and he's got the balls enough to say, "Books, old newspaper articles… This is a work of fiction."

Dante didn't believe him. "You mean, you're makin' it all up?" he says.

"Yeah. Most of it," the kid says. "I'm telling a story. The Siegel murder is just a jumping off point."

"Like through the window," Dante says, cocking his fist and moving toward him, "if you don't start givin' us the right answers."

"I'm telling you the truth," the kid says.

"Sounds like your agent's got a big mouth," Sammy says.

"Yeah," the kid says. "He's in the hospital. Got mugged."

"We know," Sammy says.

"Hey," the kid says, "if you guys don't want me to write this book… I was thinking of dropping the whole project anyway."

Sammy patted the kid on the shoulder. "Naw, go ahead and write it," he says. "We just wanted to be sure one of our guys wasn't talkin' out of school."

"Not to me!"

"Sorry we roughed you up," Sammy says as he's headin' for the door.

The kid was just happy that they were goin'. "Forget it," he says.

And, that's when I walked back into the office.

"Eddie!" Sammy says.

"Sammy!" I say.

"Oh, shit!" I hear the kid say.

"What're you doin' here?" Sammy asks.

"What're *you* doin' here?" I ask him back.

"You first," Sam says.

I pointed to the kid. "I pay him to get my name in the paper," I say.

"Your name's never *in* the paper," Sammy says.

"I know," I say. "He does a lousy job. I'm here to fire him."

All of a sudden, Dante's got a piece in his hand, and it's got a silencer on it. "Told you he was dirty," he says with this smug look on his face.

Sammy was always a reasonable guy. "Let's sit down," he says to me. "Straighten this all out."

"Sammy," I say, "I just want to fire him. Not shoot 'im."

I could tell that Dante was just itchin' to pull that trigger.

The kid, still at his desk, grabs the phone and starts to dial.

"Bad idea," Sammy says without lookin' at him, and the kid hangs up.

"Now," he says to me, "let's cut the bullshit. Tell me what's goin' on."

I make like I'm gonna sit, but then I make a grab for Dante's piece. I slug the big goon in the gut. He doubles over and the gun goes off, shattering a window. I give him an uppercut, and then I snatch the piece while he goes fallin' backward onto his ass.

The kid, I see, has taken a dive under his desk. I turn back to Sam, and he's just standin' there, pretty calm. "Now," I say, "you tell *me* what's goin' on."

"No problem, Eddie," Sammy says. "Relax!" He sits.

The kid crawls out from under the desk. "Can I, please, be excused?" he says.

"Sure, kid," I say. "Go take a leak."

The kid starts to leave, but then he hangs in the doorway.

"My people are worried, Eddie," Sammy says. "And, when I see this, what am I supposed to think?"

"You *know* I'm not a rat," I say.

"Yeah, but..." He points to the kid. "You're singin' to this putz."

"Who am I hurting?" I say. "Everybody else on Bugsy's contract is dead. Besides, I'm going to use a sudi-something."

"A pseudonym," the kid says.

"Yeah, that," I say.

I hear a *click*, and then the kid shouts, *"Eddie!"*

I spin around, and here's Dante barreling at me with a switchblade in his hand.

The kid sticks his foot out, and the big son-of-a-bitch trips over it. I give the guy a push, and he plows right into Sammy, blade and all.

Sammy gets it right in the ticker. He drops to the floor, blood spurtin' in every direction, and then he croaks.

The goon gets up and just stands there in shock. I give him a rap on the back of the head with the butt of his piece, and he goes down next to Sammy.

"Oh, Jesus!" the kid says. "Should we call an ambulance?"

"Too late," I say. "Let's get outta here."

"But, this is *my* office."

"You'd better come with me 'til this mess gets straightened out."

"I've got nothing to do with this," he says.

I look over at Dante, who's sleepin' like a baby. "You wanna tell that to the idiot there...*and* his friends"

"I see your point."

The kid grabbed his coat. We stepped out into the hallway. He shut the door, and then we headed for the elevator.

The doors to the elevator open, and guess who steps out.

It's the copper that the kid was talkin' to the other day in front of his house. And, he's got a Fed with him.

I know it's a Fed 'cause he's wearing a cheap suit.

"Mr. Goldman?" the copper says. I later find out his name is "Blanchard."

The kid looks like he's gonna faint. "Hi," he says.

The Fed, his name was "Dixon," recognizes me. "Eddie C!" he says, lookin' like the cat who'd trapped the canary.

"Who?" Blanchard, the copper, says.

"Wiseguy," Dixon, the Fed, says. "Very well connected."

"You got it wrong," I say. "I was never Made. I was just an associate."

That's when Blanchard spots the piece I'm still carryin'. So, what else can I do? I level it at 'im.

"Gun!" he shouts, but he don't move.

"Eddie!" the kid says. "What're you doing?"

"Not a good idea," the Fed says, almost in a whisper. Them Feds are calm guys.

"Kid," I say, "get their pieces."

"I don't want their guns," he says, and he starts heading back toward his office. Then, he remembers what's inside, and he stops. "Officers," he says, "I had nothing to do with…nothing… I was just writing a book, and I didn't even want to write it."

I could tell that Blanchard and the Fed didn't know what the hell he was talkin' about.

The kid just kept on goin'. "What happened in my office was not my fault," he says. "It wasn't Eddie's fault… It was an accident."

And, the kid was right. If Sammy and his goon hadn't shown up, none of this would have happened. I was just defending myself, and the kid—he saved my life.

He saved my life.

I owed him.

I couldn't ruin his.

"There's a couple of interesting guys back in the office that you might like to meet," I say. Then, I handed Blanchard the piece and raised my hands. "The kid had nuthin' to do with nuthin'."

Four hours later, after we explain what went down, the mess in the kid's office is cleaned up like it never happened, and him and me are sitting in a FBI interview room, talking with Dixon, the Fed. They even had one of them stenographers in there with us.

"Eddie," the Fed says, "you cooperate with us, and we'll put you and your mother in the Witness Protection Program."

"What about my cats?" I say. "Can they come, too?"

"I don't know," he says. "We'll see."

"What about me?" the kid says. "Do I have to go into the Witness Protection Program, too?"

I say, "Maybe we can go in together, kid."

I can tell he don't like that idea.

"I don't think that will be necessary, Mr. Goldman," the Fed says. "After all, you don't really know anything about the inner workings of the Mob, do you?"

"He don't know shit," I say.

"So," the Fed says to the kid, "you're no threat to them."

"Can I still write my book?" the kid says.

"What the hell you gonna write about?" I ask.

"How about the last few days?" he says.

"That might work," I say.

"Okay, Eddie," the Fed says, "how about it?"

Actually, Witness Protection was pretty good deal for me 'cause, 'cept for Dante, the goon, 'bout the only people I could sing about were all dead and buried. But, I wasn't goin' to make it easy on 'em. "First, we talk about my cats?" I said.

They sent the kid home, and he wrote his book. I hear it was a best seller.

They turned Dante. With Sammy's killing hanging over him, that was easy. And, he knew a hell of a lot more of what was goin' on with the wiseguys those days than I did. Then, they put him into Witness Protection and I have no idea where they sent him.

Me, my mother and my three cats got sent to Montana.

Montana's an okay place...if you like cows.

I kinda miss the cats on the corner back in Agoura Hills.

The kid, he promised that he'd feed 'em for me every night.

Last I heard, he's still doin' it.

○

About the Author

Michael B. Druxman is a veteran Hollywood screenwriter whose credits include *Cheyenne Warrior* with Kelly Preston; *Dillinger and Capone* starring Martin Sheen and F. Murray Abraham, and *The Doorway* with Roy Scheider, which he also directed.

He is also a prolific playwright; his one-person play, *Jolson*, having had numerous productions around the country. Other produced stage credits include one-person plays about Clark Gable, Carole Lombard, Spencer Tracy and Orson Welles. These plays have been individually published under the collective title of *The Hollywood Legends*.

Additionally, Mr. Druxman is the author of fourteen other published books, including several nonfiction works about Hollywood, its movies, and the people who make them (e.g., *Basil Rathbone: His Life and His Films, Make It Again, Sam: A Survey of Movie Remakes, One Good Film Deserves Another: A Survey of Movie Sequels, Merv* [Griffin] and *The Musical: From Broadway to Hollywood*).

He has written two novels, *Nobody Drowns in Mineral Lake* and *Shadow Watcher*, plus the humorous revisionist history, *Once Upon a Time in Hollywood: From the Secret Files of Harry Pennypacker*, and *Family Secret*, a non-fiction book co-authored with Warren Hull, which reveals the true facts behind the 1947 murder of mobster "Bugsy" Siegel in Beverly Hills.

An acknowledged Hollywood historian, he has also written television documentaries and has been interviewed for various retrospective featurettes that have accompanied DVD releases of classic films (e.g. *The Maltese Falcon*, etc.)

Mr. Druxman is a former Hollywood publicist of 35 years experience who has represented many film and television stars, as well as noted directors, producers and composers. One of his Academy Award campaigns is often mentioned in books dealing with Oscar's history.

He has taught various dramatic writing and film appreciation courses in an adult university and is the author of *How to Write a Story...Any Story: The Art of Storytelling*, which has been used as a text in several colleges.

A native of Seattle who graduated from Garfield High School and the University of Washington, Mr. Druxman moved with his wife, Sandy, from Los Angeles to Austin, TX in 2009.

His memoir, *My Forty-Five Years in Hollywood and How I Escaped Alive*, was published in 2010 by Bear Manor Media.

.